# PENELOPE

# PENELOPE

Marilyn Kaye

ST. MARTIN'S GRIFFIN ✖ NEW YORK

PENELOPE. Copyright © 2007 by Penelope Productions, LLC. Introduction copyright © 2007 by Reese Witherspoon. All rights reserved. Printed in the United States of America. For information, address St. Martin's Press, 175 Fifth Avenue, New York, N.Y. 10010.

www.stmartins.com

ISBN-13: 978-0-312-37559-1
ISBN-10: 0-312-37559-X

10  9  8  7  6  5  4  3

*For the team: Thomas Clerc, Emilie Grimaud,*
*Augustin Clerc, Marion Grimaud, and the cocaptains,*
*Isabelle and Hervé*

# Introduction

I loved reading fairy tales as a child—or better yet, having them read to me—and now my daughter loves them too! The adventures of those beleaguered princesses, so often the youngest, most beautiful, and least appreciated, were magical. Fairy tales tell us who we are and how to live. That's why they are so powerful. It's not often that a brand-new tale appears in the world. So imagine my surprise and delight when I discovered . . . *Penelope!*

Sprung from the brilliantly original brain of Leslie Caveny, *Penelope* appeared on my desk one fine spring day. I loved the story from the moment I read it, and Penelope came to life in my imagination long before she stepped on-screen.

There are so many things I love about *Penelope*: a terrific plot, great characters, a beautiful world. But most of all, I love the message. *Penelope* is the inspiring story of a girl who is told by the people closest to her that she isn't good enough. Born with the face of a pig due to an ancient curse that had nothing to do with her, Penelope is kept hidden away in her parents' house and is taught to wait—to wait until her prince comes along and rescues her, to wait until she is pretty enough to go out into the world, to wait for her life to begin.

Eventually, Penelope gets tired of waiting and takes things into her own hands. Breaking free from her family, she heads out into the world to experience life on her own terms, finding friendship, adventure, and fun along the way. Penelope ultimately learns that she is pretty great the way she is, and it is that confidence and self-acceptance that prove to be life changing.

I've been all over the world and met so many people, and I've come to discover that each and every one of us has insecurities. Young or old, short or tall, we all have something we wish we could change about ourselves. Sometimes we let those insecurities define who we are and get in the way of all the great things we could accomplish. Penelope teaches us to rise above our fears, to embrace the things that make us unique, and to celebrate our individuality. She faces the world with fearlessness and wonder.

I hope this story inspires you to try to be a little more like Penelope, and to learn to love what is truly unique about yourself.

Enjoy the book!

—Reese Witherspoon

# Chapter One

Jake always knew where to find me.

He'd been with our family since, well, forever, and he knew our routines. He also knew our habits, our tastes, our foibles and our problems—in fact, he probably knew the Wilherns better than we knew ourselves. Actually, that wasn't so remarkable given that there were only three Wilherns in the house—my mother, my father, and me—and none of us were all that complicated.

In any case, he was familiar with my weekday schedule (which didn't vary that much from my week-end schedule). Breakfast at 8:30. From 9:00 to 10:00, I listened to French tapes and practiced conjugating verbs. That pluperfect subjunctive was a killer.

From 10:00 to 10:45, I was on the stationary bike or the treadmill or some other kind of aerobic instrument of endurance/torture. I wasn't really a sporty type, but I believed that exercise was very important, particularly for people who didn't get out much.

After my workout, I showered and changed, and at

11:00 I watched my favorite TV soap opera, where the characters led lives much more interesting than mine. And at noon I read the newspaper, which was filled with stories about people whose lives were much worse than mine (not that I enjoyed knowing that their lives were sad, but it kept any hint of self-pity at bay). Lunch was at 12:45. By 2:30 every day, I was in the solarium-slash-greenhouse, and that was where Jake came to collect me.

When he arrived, I was in the middle of a delicate procedure, dividing my bird-of-paradise in preparation for transplanting. This required concentration—I had to separate the roots and try very hard not to break them—so I wasn't too pleased when Jake appeared in the doorway and made his announcement.

"Miss Penelope, your three o'clock is here."

"Already?" I cried in dismay.

"Well, it *is* three o'clock," the butler pointed out. He gazed around the solarium. "Your plants look lovely, Miss Penelope."

"Thank you, Jake."

"How unfortunate that others don't have the pleasure of seeing them."

"Mm." Reluctantly, I put the bird-of-paradise aside and pulled off my plastic gloves. I was really in no mood for what was about to happen, but I also knew there was no point in trying to put it off.

"Oh, and your mother would like to see you before the meeting," Jake added.

This was nothing new. Mother always wanted to see me before the meetings to give me an update on the candidate and a little pep talk.

My mother, Jessica Wilhern, was in her usual place at the dining table, which was littered with folders, photos, and resumes. With her was Wanda, who'd been hired seven years ago as a live-in consultant to work with her on this important project.

"Darling," my mother trilled in the slightly breathless voice she used to encourage an upbeat and positive attitude. "I think we have an interesting prospect here. Wanda, tell her."

Wanda nodded. With her usual efficiency, she had all the facts on hand. "*Very* interesting. Palmer Metcalf, aged twenty-five. Your age, Penelope."

I spoke through my teeth. "Yes, Wanda, I know how old I am."

Wanda ignored my feeble attempt at sarcasm. "He has excellent credentials. Livingstone Prep, Dartmouth. Junior partner, Mitchell and Swinson, Securities. Member, Clearwater Town and Country Club. Country house in Woodbridge. And by the way, these are the *Providence* Metcalfs, not the Boston ones. The Boston ones didn't arrive until way after the *Mayflower,* at least ten years. And rumor has it they sailed tourist."

I made a small effort to appear mildly impressed. "Dartmouth. That's in New Hampshire, right?"

"His father's on the *board of trustees*!" my mother added excitedly. "He has connections. Your children can go to Ivy League schools!"

"Palmer spent a year studying at the Sorbonne in Paris," Wanda continued.

My mother was now over the moon. "He lived in France, Penelope! France! You could speak French together!"

"Penelope Metcalf," Wanda said experimentally. "It has a nice ring."

Feigning enthusiasm was getting harder and harder. I was so sick of all this. And I really wanted to get back to those bird-of-paradise roots. "Okay, okay, he's perfect. He's in the music room?"

"Of course, darling, where else? Look!"

I glanced at the other end of the dining room, where a loveseat and small coffee table were waiting for me by a one-way window. Through this window I could see into the music room, but anyone in the music room would see a mirror. I walked right past the furniture to the door leading directly into the music room.

Wanda gasped and my mother shrieked, "Penelope, what are you doing?"

I ignored them both and opened the door. A nice-looking young man, very preppy in a tweed jacket, and presumably Palmer Metcalf, immediately rose from the sofa and turned to face me.

*"Bonjour,"* I said.

His mouth opened but no words came out. His face said it all for him.

It didn't surprise me, since I'd seen the look before, with slight variations. It could range from disbelief to total shock, from distaste to disgust. Sometimes I saw fear, or even downright horror.

*"Je m'appelle Penelope."*

He was already edging toward the door.

*"Comment allez-vous?"*

He'd recovered sufficiently to stutter, "I, uh . . . I can't . . . I have to be somewhere."

*"Au revoir,"* I said.

He'd made it to the hallway, where Jake was waiting with papers for him to sign. I went back into the dining room to face the wrath of Jessica Wilhern and company. Wanda was shaking her head in dismay while my mother expressed her displeasure more audibly.

"Penelope, what is the matter with you?" she shrieked. "Why did you do that? You know better, you can't just go out there! You can't just spring yourself on a man like that! You can't blame him for being shocked!"

"This is completely unacceptable, Jessica," Wanda fumed. "How do you expect me to do my job when Penelope won't cooperate?"

Another voice was heard. "Oh, don't be so hard on her, ladies."

I hadn't even realized my father was in the room. Franklin Wilhern could do that—appear and disappear without anyone noticing. I appreciated his sweet, worried expression though, and I smiled at him. Jessica and Wanda ignored his comment and continued their tirade.

"Penelope, you have to let a young man *know* you before you show yourself," my mother pleaded. "Do you think I let your father see my mole before we were married? No, of course not, he had to love me first, then he could accept the fact that I wasn't flawless. Isn't that right, Franklin?"

He nodded. "You're not flawless, Jessica."

Jessica went on. "You have to reveal what's inside, your true self, your beautiful self. A man has to realize that you're a delightful, charming, intelligent young woman before he sees that . . . before he knows that . . ."

She was having trouble saying it so I helped her out and finished the sentence for her.

"That I have the face of a pig?"

"Oh, Penelope!" she wailed.

"Sorry, folks, I've got a bird-of-paradise waiting for me," I said. "Gotta go."

As I walked out of the dining room, I could hear them continuing without me. Wanda, threatening to quit her job as professional matchmaker. My mother, accusing me of ruining my own life (and hers in the process). And beneath the voices of the two women came the faint words of my poor, dear father, pleading with them, as usual.

"It's not her fault. Don't blame Penelope. It's my fault, it's all my fault."

# Chapter Two

You'd think I'd be used to it by now. I wasn't, and I doubted that I ever would be. It was always painful and demoralizing.

Normally, at a moment like this, I would go back to the peace and quiet of the solarium. Plants were my passion in life, and they comforted me when I was tense or depressed or angry. But at that moment, I was tense *and* depressed *and* angry, and even my beloved plants couldn't alleviate all that. In fact, I was more afraid my wretched mood would cause irreparable damage to the innocent plants.

So I went to my room, which wasn't a bad place to hide out and console myself. It had everything one could wish for in a bedroom. Lavish furniture, including a canopy bed fit for a princess. Fresh flowers everywhere, magnificent art on the walls. Walk-in closets filled with clothes I'd found in catalogs and on Internet shopping sites. Shelves of handbags and shoes. Drawers packed with jewelry. I liked fashion—I'd developed my own style, and every season my closets went through a complete overhaul. I never had to worry about being seen in last season's styles. Mainly because I was never seen.

And I was surrounded by all the entertainment possibilities. Wide-screen flat TV, the finest stereo system in the world, thousands of CDs and DVDs, video game systems.

Not to mention my exercise alcove, which included a treadmill, bike, a rowing machine, and a climbing wall. The climbing wall was my favorite. I had to put on special equipment, organize the ropes, then stretch and strain to get from one foothold to the next, and it took a long time to get to the top where I reached—nothing. All I could do then was come back down. It seemed to me like a metaphor for my life—I kept moving but I went nowhere.

The only thing a stranger might think was missing from the room was a mirror. But my mother had always felt it would be way too depressing for me to encounter my reflection on a daily basis.

I *did* have a mirror she didn't know about. It was in a powder compact that I'd stolen from her handbag years ago. It was very small, but I didn't require a full-length mirror to remind me why I didn't have a normal life. Not that I ever needed a reminder at all. When you had the face of a pig, you never forgot it.

It didn't matter if I changed the angle of the mirror,

or tilted my head, or looked at myself in profile. Even if I lowered my eyelids to blur the image, there was no possible way to miss the feature that had kept me a prisoner all my life, the feature that drove away Palmer Metcalf (among many others): the huge, fleshy, prominent snout that had marked me since birth.

Of course, there were other parts to my face—the snout wasn't my only feature, though it certainly commanded the most attention. I had eyes, and I had to admit, they weren't half bad. They were big, chocolate-brown, and adorned with unusually long lashes.

Mouthwise, I was in pretty good shape, too. The lips had a nice shape, not too full, not too thin, and when parted they revealed perfectly straight white teeth. I'd lucked out with my complexion, too. It was fair without being pale, despite the fact that I was always indoors, and I didn't even have to resort to fake tanning lotions. I'd never had acne, and my cheeks were imbued with a pretty rosy blush.

I also had a very good figure. With all the time I had available for exercise, it was easy to maintain. And my hair was particularly nice. The rich deep brown was my very own color, and there were delicate waves that culminated in curls that bounced around my shoulders.

There *was* a small problem with my ears, which had some pig-like elements. Fortunately, however, my hair kept them concealed. But nothing could conceal the snout, and no matter how many lovely physical qualities I had, they were all reduced to negligible by this protuberance.

And as much as I tried not to feel sorry for myself, at moments like this I felt like I was entitled to wallow in a little self-pity. Whenever this mood hit, I indulged myself in a certain routine.

From my bookcase, I extracted the Wilhern Family Scrapbook, settled myself in a comfortable rocking chair, and opened it.

I turned to a particular page and gazed at an old sepia print, a family portrait. Stern-faced Wilherns posed stiffly in dark serious clothes, Victorian style. This particular photo was probably taken around 1860. There were five young men in the photo, but my attention was focused on one: my great-great-great-grandfather, Ralph Wilhern.

I blamed him.

# Chapter Three

Ralph was not the oldest nor the youngest Wilhern brother—he was right in the middle, with two older brothers and two younger brothers. Of the five young men, he was not the smartest. He wasn't the best-looking Wilhern, either. Nor was he the most athletic, or the most creative, or the most ambitious. No one would ever have called him driven—he tended to indolence, he was somewhat shy, and he was easily intimidated and influenced by his parents and his brothers, even the two younger ones. As far as personality and charm went, he didn't stand out.

He was aware of his flaws, because his parents and brothers were always reminding him. Nowadays, a shrink would say he had something of an inferiority complex. But neuroses hadn't been invented yet—at least, the idea of them hadn't reached the world of the Wilherns—so Ralph had to deal with his inadequacies the only way he knew how. He became a romantic.

He read romantic poetry and romantic novels and he

engaged in a lot of romantic fantasy. Real romance didn't play a big part in his world. He knew what was expected of him: to finish school, to go into the family business (which had something to do with using money to make more money), to refrain from actions that might in some way injure the respectable reputation of the family, to marry a good woman from a good family, and to perpetuate the Wilhern name. He could manage most of these responsibilities, but there was one that gave Ralph some trouble: finding a wife.

He didn't have any problem meeting eligible women. From the age of eighteen, he had attended coming-out balls and other special occasions designed for the sole purpose of introducing the young men and women of a certain class. The women were of different shapes and sizes and appearance, but they were all moral and upright, well groomed and well mannered. Ralph's problem was that they didn't appeal to his romantic nature. He thought they were dull.

If he'd been a little more ambitious, or had the tiniest spark of imagination, he might have left home, traveled, gone beyond the small circle of local aristocracy. But Ralph never even considered the possibility that there were other options in life. He could only fantasize and wish for romance to come knocking at his door.

By the time his older and even his younger brothers had married or become betrothed, the Wilhern patriarch and matriarch were becoming concerned, and so more effort was put into Ralph's social schedule. He found himself escorting Sibyl, Caroline, Elizabeth, and every other woman who met the basic criteria of family and class. Dutifully, he obliged, but none of the women could fulfill his fantasy of romance. And then, he met Clara.

As a large and wealthy family, the Wilherns employed a substantial number of servants. Most of them lived in sparse rooms in the mansion's attic, though a few came daily from local farms. Like his brothers, Ralph wasn't terribly aware of them, and he never thought about them. When he put on a clean, pressed, white shirt every morning, he might have experienced a brief moment of satisfaction at the sense of well-being it provided, but it never occurred to him that some actual human being had washed and ironed it. He might exclaim about the tastiness of the Sunday roast chicken and not give a thought to the fact that someone had cooked it.

Like most people of his class, he lived a comfortable life without thinking about why or how it had come to be so comfortable. And he couldn't tell the difference between Mary who did the washing or Sally who swept the floors or Martha who made the beds. Or Clara, who chopped the vegetables for the meals that Cook produced.

But one Sunday afternoon, Clara turned Ralph's comfortable world upside down.

The family had just finished their extensive Sunday lunch. While the food had been excellent and plentiful,

Ralph was feeling somewhat empty. At church that morning, he'd sat with Sibyl Harrington. His parents then spent the entire meal extolling Sibyl's virtues, and urging Ralph to ask Sibyl's father for her hand in marriage.

Ralph didn't have any problem with Sibyl. She was no different from Caroline or Elizabeth or any of the other potential wives. He'd actually begun to contemplate complying with his parents' desire. He was thinking that perhaps he was a fool to long for romance and joy, the passions that were obliquely described in his favorite novels. Perhaps such feelings as these were reserved for poetry alone and didn't exist in the real world.

Restless and depressed, he decided to go for a walk, something that would have disturbed the family if they'd known, since Sunday walks were not a part of their routine. The weekly promenade was always taken through the Great Park on late Saturday afternoon, when all the others of their kind did their promenade. To walk at any other time suggested that one could not afford a carriage.

Fortunately for Ralph, no one knew he was about to take a Sunday walk, since the after-luncheon ritual on Sundays was a long nap. The other members of his family were all asleep when he slipped out of the house. And in order not to be spotted by anyone who might pass him in a carriage and then report his peculiar behavior to his parents, he decided to do something seriously bizarre: he would take a walk in the woods.

He had been in the woods once before, as a boy, on a nature hike led by the local schoolmaster, who could provide the Latin names for vegetation and identify poisonous mushrooms. So he knew that there was a path, and that there were no wild animals. What he didn't know was that a certain kitchen maid from his own household often spent Sunday afternoons picking wildflowers there. She also searched out herbs for her mother, a noted local witch (not notable to Ralph, though, since, like all the Wilherns, he only knew his own kind).

As Ralph ambled down the narrow path through the woods, his senses (not particularly acute) picked up on a sound that wasn't being made by birds. It took more than a minute for him to realize that what he was hearing was singing, an activity that was considered inappropriate on a Sunday (except for hymns at church) and that was never encountered in the Wilhern household anyway.

Curious (an attitude also unusual for Ralph), he followed the sound of the voice, and eventually discovered its source. At some distance from his trail, he saw a young woman in a small clearing.

The women in the Wilhern social circle had certain common elements of appearance. Their hair was worn in the popular sculpted style known as a pompadour, where each lock was fastened with some sort of pin that held it in place. Perhaps it was unfastened at night when the women went to sleep, but Ralph wouldn't have known about that. Faces were kept out of the sun, and therefore pale, and cosmetics were only used by women of ill repute. The women they knew socially all seemed to have the same type of body too—fat or thin, they wore stiffly wired corsets that forced their bodies into a similar shape. All items of clothing were in dark colors, and designed to cover every inch of flesh.

So one could only imagine Ralph's shock when he saw Clara in the woods. She was not in the black uniform worn by all female servants in the Wilhern household, nor was her hair pulled back in the requisite tight bun. Thus, Ralph could not recognize her as a servant (especially since he never bothered to look into any servants' faces), but he had to be aware that she was not of his kind.

Clara was a slight, wispy girl with delicate limbs and a tiny waist. She wasn't a great beauty, but her face had a sweet prettiness. Her eyes were blue, and her hair was fair and long, hanging without restriction almost to her waist. In Ralph's eyes, she looked like a nymph, a sprite, the kind of untamed fairy-like creature he found in poetry.

Her feet were bare, and she wore neither hat nor gloves. She was dressed in a skirt and top of some very thin material that was practically transparent, and the warmth of the sun had provoked her to roll up her sleeves. She was showing a great deal more feminine flesh than was normally seen in public, but it wasn't at all provocative. The word that immediately came to

Ralph's mind as a way to describe her was *romantic*. A word he'd never expected to be able to apply to something alive and real.

She appeared to be in the process of gathering wildflowers, and as she picked them she sang.

"Let me linger in the valley with my own true love, let us dance in the moonlight under starry skies above . . ."

He ventured off the path, stepping on a twig that cracked loudly. The sound made the girl jump and she turned in his direction.

Although, as noted earlier, Ralph wasn't the best-looking of the Wilherns, his appearance wasn't unattractive. He was tall and slender, with dark wavy hair, heavy-lidded eyes, and generally patrician features, although a large droopy moustache hid a weak chin. He was well dressed in the fashion of the day and well groomed, unarmed (with the exception of a walking stick), and he presented to Clara a figure that was not at all threatening.

And yet, she was alarmed, and dropped her flowers.

"Sir!" she gasped. "Oh, sir, I'm so terribly sorry, forgive me."

He found her subservience oddly appealing. "What are you sorry for?"

"Why . . . because I have disturbed your walk, sir."

"Nonsense," Ralph said. "It is I who have disturbed your flower gathering. And why do you call me 'sir'?"

"Because you are my master, sir."

He rather liked the sound of that. "Are you speaking in a romantic context, miss?"

"No, sir. I work for your family. I am Clara, the kitchen maid. I assist Cook."

Ralph pouted. Kitchen maid had a decidedly unromantic flavor.

"I chop the vegetables," Clara added.

He raised his eyebrows hopefully. "Is it you who creates the little flowers from radishes?"

"Yes, sir."

*That* lifted his spirits. He'd always thought those radishes looked like little rosebuds, and rosebuds were certainly romantic.

"So your name is Clara," he said. He rolled the name around in his mouth. "Cl-a-a-ra." Well, it wasn't Dulcinea or Desdemona but at least it wasn't Gertrude. "And do you know my name?"

"Yes, sir. Mister Wilhern."

"There are five Mister Wilherns in the house, six including Father. Do you know which Mister Wilhern I am?"

She hesitated, and he thought he knew why. He'd always disliked his first name. There were romantic names for men, like Edmund or Jonathan. But *Ralph* . . . he couldn't have known in 1860 that it would one day become a slang expression for vomiting, but perhaps he was prescient, because he sensed an unpleasant connotation.

"It would not be appropriate for I, a servant girl, to use your first name, sir."

"Then I shall give you a special name to call me, Clara. I am . . ." He ran through the names of heroes in his latest readings. "You may call me Roderigo."

"Roderigo, sir?"

"Just Roderigo, not Roderigo sir. We cannot have a proper relationship if you call me sir."

"Relationship, sir? I mean, Roderigo?"

"Yes, my dear. I believe you are the woman I have been waiting for all my life." He took her hand and kissed it.

Clara was very young, barely sixteen, and she had little experience of men. Her mother saw to that, keeping her close in the little hovel they shared in the woods, only allowing her out for her job in the Big House, and to gather the herbs and bits of animal remains necessary for spells. She tried to teach Clara the tricks of her trade, but she had come to realize that Clara showed little natural talent for witchcraft, and had decided that her daughter's pretty face and sweet nature would be her ticket to the good life. At that moment in time, she had her eye on a local blacksmith, which would be a big step up from the family's current social status.

When Clara came home with news of Roderigo, her pet name for one of the Wilhern heirs, the witch was astonished and delighted. Never could she have expected her slightly dim daughter, who had a tendency to break out in rashes, to rise so high on the social ladder. She immediately went to work on preparing various potions and spells to keep the flames of love burning.

But there didn't seem to be any real need for her to utilize magic. Before she'd even had a chance to administer any potions or cast any spells, Roderigo/Ralph and Clara had joined together and become inseparable (except, of course, for when she was chopping her vegetables—Ralph didn't know where the kitchen was located in the Wilhern mansion and it would have been unseemly for him to make an appearance there anyway).

They would meet in the evenings, when the other members of the family had retired to their private bedrooms. Ralph would slip out of the house and meet her in the clearing, where she would sing that little song she liked, and they would follow its instructions, dancing in the moonlight under the stars. And they would lie in the grass, holding each other, and he would recite poetry she didn't understand (but then, neither did he).

He'd found what was missing in his life. The Sibyls and Carolines of the world, those proper, corseted young ladies, would never sing love songs, or dance, or run barefoot through the woods, or engage in certain other activities that Ralph and Clara enjoyed immensely. He thought about her incessantly, which made him smile and caused his mother to be constantly inquiring as to his digestion.

In time, she asked him to meet her mother, and he was enthralled with the notion. Having never met a real witch, he envisioned someone fantastical. He'd read his childhood fairy tales so he knew she would not be particularly attractive, but still, she was magical, and that was romantic.

He wasn't prepared, however, for the extreme ugliness of Clara's mother. Emerging from the rundown wooden shack was an old, bent-over woman, with a pimpled nose, a jutting chin, and long wild gray hair, leaning on a crooked stick. He was much relieved to learn that her appearance was a by-product of her career, that every spell cast left a mark on the spellcaster, which was why working witches always looked like she did. She assured Ralph that Clara had absolutely no inclination to become a witch herself, and therefore would never look like her mother.

Mother and daughter seemed to have a pleasant relationship, although the witch kept telling Clara she was becoming plump. As weeks passed, Clara's stomach continued to grow. Eventually, they all figured out why, and Ralph asked the witch for Clara's hand. The witch told him he could have all of her daughter's body parts, and Ralph happily went to convey the glorious news to his parents and brothers.

The Wilherns gathered in the library for the announcement, and Ralph, after only a few wrong turns, was able to make it to the kitchen to fetch Clara. Clara, however, was mashing potatoes and at a particularly crucial point, and said she would join them all as soon as she was through. Ralph alone met the family in the library.

"Mother, Father, dear brothers, I hope you will share in my joy as I tell you I have decided to marry."

The brothers gave a rousing cheer, and his mother sighed. "At last." The father nodded his approval and said, "Very good, my boy, Sibyl will make an excellent wife."

"Oh, I'm not marrying Sibyl," Ralph said.

"Caroline?" his mother asked. "Elizabeth?"

"No," Ralph said.

One of the brothers asked, "Do we know the woman?"

Ralph was enjoying the suspense. "My bride-to-be is no stranger to this household."

The lumps in the mashed potatoes were being unusually tenacious that day, so Clara never made it to the library. It was just as well, as she might not have appreciated the family reaction.

"I am going to marry Clara."

"Clara?" his father repeated. "Clara?" He turned to his wife. "Do we know a Clara?"

"Clara who?" Ralph's mother asked him.

It dawned on Ralph that he'd never learned Clara's family name. "Clara! The maid, the one who works in the kitchen with Cook. The one who chops the vegetables. Mother, you're always saying how much you relish those little radish roses. Clara has assured me that even when she becomes Mrs. Ralph Wilhern, she will continue to make those little roses. Just for special occasions, of course."

None of the Wilherns, especially Ralph, was known for having a great sense of humor, which may have explained why the sudden eruption of laughter made no sense to him whatsoever.

"I am pleased to see that this news makes you happy," he said uncertainly.

"Very funny, my boy, very funny," his father exclaimed. "A good joke."

"Highly amusing," his mother agreed.

"Meet my sister-in-law, the scullery maid," his eldest brother chortled. "I must remember to tell this story at the Club."

"Yes, I was thinking perhaps we could hold the wedding reception there," Ralph said, and that set off another round of guffaws.

It took Ralph a while before he caught on to the joke. Ultimately, it was left to his father to explain that a Wilhern did not, could not, would not marry a servant girl. It wasn't done. The rules of society would not permit it. A century or more later, a duke might marry a nanny, a millionaire could marry his secretary, but back then the mere thought of a blue-blooded Wilhern exchanging vows with a member of a lower class was unthinkable.

Ralph was surprised. He thought he knew the codes of conduct, but apparently some of them hadn't sunk in. And although Clara had touched his romantic side, he really wasn't a rebel. He wasn't the type to flout convention in a really public way. Maybe his father threatened to cut him off without a dime, I wasn't sure. But it didn't really matter—Ralph Wilhern agreed to uphold the family's standing, and asked Sibyl to marry him instead. (She turned him down, but Caroline, who would have married the Hunchback of Notre Dame to get out of her family home, accepted him.)

And poor, despondent, pregnant Clara threw herself down a well.

That was the end of Clara, but it wasn't the end of the story. Needless to say, when the witch learned of her daughter's suicide, she was devastated; and when she learned the reasons for it, she was furious at the Wilhern family. And on one dark, moonless night, she hobbled over to the Wilhern mansion with a special mix of herbs, spices, and one finely ground hog's tail. Leaning on her crooked stick, she recited an incantation of her own invention and sprinkled her nasty little marinade around the house. Then she raised the stick, pointed it toward the house, and declared her revenge on the family.

You'd think, in all fairness, she would focus her curse on Ralph, who had dumped her daughter. Or simply extend the curse to the parents who forbid the marriage and the brothers who laughed.

But the curse she placed on the family had far-reaching repercussions—namely, me. Because what really irked the witch was the whole class thing, the idea of this uppity aristocracy who considered others—like servants and witches—to be way beneath them. So she cursed them with something that would hurt a random member of their blue-blooded dynasty.

The witch declared that the next female born into the Wilhern family would have the face of a pig. And the curse could only be lifted when someone of their own kind, a true blue blood, would claim her till death they did part. Only when an aristocrat could accept the pig-girl as she was would the curse be broken.

It was a pretty nasty curse, but given what happened to her daughter, you couldn't really blame her.

Considering that all this happened more than a hundred and fifty years ago, you'd think the curse would have manifested itself long before my birth. Unfortunately—for me, at least—the Wilhern men seemed to have been abundantly endowed with y chromosomes or something. For a hundred years, only male progeny were produced. Then, around fifty years ago, my great-uncle Leonard Wilhern and his wife, Ella, had a baby girl, Isabel.

Now, this was before the time when there were tests that determined a baby's sex before birth, so all Wilherns were tense just before a birth, though the level of anxiety had diminished somewhat over the years as people believed less and less in the power of witches and witchcraft. Still, the odds were that the Wilherns couldn't produce only boys forever, and Uncle Leonard in particular was apprehensive.

Interestingly enough, according to my father, who was a child at the time, Aunt Ella didn't seem to be worried about the curse at all. She laughed off the legend and made jokes about having a litter of piglets. The more superstitious members of the family feared she was actually inviting the evil eye into her home.

So everyone was greatly relieved when baby Isabel was born a perfect little girl, and the curse of the witch was dismissed as nonsense. What few knew was the fact that Isabel was never at risk—Auntie Ella had been having an affair with the chauffeur. There wasn't a drop of Wilhern blood in that pretty child.

So it was up to the next generation to fulfill the witch's promise. I was never sure if my mother knew about the curse when she married my father. Maybe by then everyone had forgotten all about it.

Surprise.

# Chapter Four

When Uncle Leonard learned of my birth, and my snout, he finally realized that his beloved wife Ella had deceived him all those many years earlier. Inconsolable, he threw himself out a window of their penthouse apartment. My mother always said that was a lucky break—the scandal of his suicide took some of the attention away from the stories and rumors about me.

There were a lot of pictures of my parents from before I was born. The Wilherns were socially prominent, and Jessica and Franklin Wilhern were a popular couple, invited everywhere to every significant occasion. In practically every photo, my mother wore a glamorous designer dress, with jewels, furs, all the usual stuff. My father looked very debonair, in beautifully tailored suits, sometimes tuxedos. There were pictures of them at balls, at horse races, at opening nights, receptions for visiting royalty, all kinds of elegant events. They'd be holding martini glasses, champagne flutes, long bejeweled cigarette holders. They might be dancing, surrounded by other beautiful people.

There was only one photo of me in the scrapbook. I was in the arms of a tense-looking Jessica with a mournful-faced Franklin standing just behind her. My baby blanket had been artfully arranged to cover my face.

My birth had been devastating for both of them, but especially for my mother. She'd been having a natural childbirth, but the minute I emerged and she saw my face, heavy-duty medication was required.

Needless to say, once my mother recovered from her initial hysteria, the first order of business was to make me normal. My parents explored every possible remedy for my condition. But that old witch was no dummy— she must have foreseen advances in cosmetic surgery and worked her curse accordingly. Surgeons told my parents that the carotid artery ran directly through the snout, uh, nose, and any attempt at modification would result in my death. I often wondered if my mother had been tempted. Interestingly enough, the only other item in the scrapbook that referred to me was my obituary notice from a local newspaper.

*Jessica and Franklin Wilhern announce with deep sorrow the untimely death of their infant daughter, Penelope . . .*

Of course, there was a perfectly good explanation

for this. My mother had been determined to keep my existence a secret, but too many people had been present at the delivery, and we were a prominent family. Rumors of the birth of a pig-girl got around, and tabloid journalists came calling. Between my parents and Jake, they were stopped in their tracks, and eventually most lost interest when rumors of a fish-boy with fins popped up in a nearby county.

But there was one particularly persistent journalist, a man named Lemon, who worked for the sleaziest of the sleazy rags. Somehow this fellow managed to get himself inside our house, and he actually confronted my mother in the kitchen with me in her arms.

He must have caught her in a particularly bad mood. Jessica went into a wild frenzy, and she lashed out, striking him in the face with a kitchen utensil. You wouldn't think a soup ladle could do much damage, but later she learned that he'd lost an eye as a result of the attack. My guess was that this had to be one of the few joyful moments she'd experienced since my birth.

But now that my existence had been (almost) confirmed—Lemon didn't get a good shot of me—she knew he'd be back, and more reporters would be coming, too. She could only think of one way to ward them off.

So my death was faked, an empty coffin was buried, or cremated, I was never sure which.

My father told me it was pretty awful for him. He

wasn't much of an actor, and although his natural expression was always a little mournful, people thought he seemed less than overcome with grief at the death of his only child. My mother assured everyone it was due to his stiff-upper-lip Wilhern upbringing, and she tried to make up for it by wailing like a banshee.

So there were no more pictures of me in the scrapbook, and not many of my parents, either. They'd stopped entertaining, since they didn't dare let any guests into the house for fear they might stumble across me. And they wouldn't go out; because they couldn't trust babysitters not to spread rumors. They could have left me in the house with Jake, but they still rarely went out. My mother was always afraid that my father might have a drink or two, slip up, and mention me. Besides, accepting invitations meant that eventually they would have to reciprocate.

So I grew up imprisoned in a gilded cage, the Wilhern mansion. Hidden from the world, I had no playmates. I wouldn't say I was deprived—I had all the material things, plus nannies and tutors to provide me with company. Anyone who met me had to sign a gag order, and I often wondered if my parents resorted to bribery or threats to enforce it. Or maybe they simply had every one of these tutors assassinated when they left their jobs.

My earliest memories were of my mother saying, "Don't worry, darling, this is not you. You are not your nose. This is not your real face, it's the face of your great-great-great-grandfather. You are somebody else inside. And someday, you'll see the real Penelope." Whenever she encountered little Penelope gazing in wonderment at her reflection, she went into her little speech. It became a mantra: "Your face is not your face." I would hear the story of the curse again, which I already knew by heart, and then she would remind me for the zillionth time that the creature I saw in the reflection wasn't the real me.

This was the way I lived. As a young child, I was a princess, dressed up beautifully every morning and treated by Jake with the kind of respect no child deserves to get. I would have my lessons with the tutor, and when lessons were finished, I played in my room. My parents spared no expense in providing me with a play-worthy room—there were sandboxes and wading pools, dolls and toys, a swing that hung from the ceiling. I would sit on it and sail across the room, from one end to the other, and pretend to be flying. Then there was dinner, and bath and bedtime.

I was allowed out in public once a year, on Halloween. Every year I would dress up differently, as a fairy, a cowgirl, a ballerina, the usual Halloween costumes (though never a witch, for obvious reasons). The main requirement for the costume was a mask that would completely cover my face. Jake would take me trick-or-treating, but I was never allowed to join in the groups of children going from house to house together. Any action that could lead to a friendship was strictly forbidden. Needless to say, Halloween became and remained my all-time favorite holiday.

Was I lonely? I suppose so, though maybe I didn't realize it at the time. After all, I didn't know any other way of life existed.

At bedtime, my mother would recite her "your face is not your face" mantra. She usually followed this up by singing "Some Day My Prince Will Come," from the Disney version of *Snow White and the Seven Dwarfs*. Then my father would read me special versions of traditional fairy tales that he had rewritten just for me. My favorite was *Handsome and the Beastie*.

"Once upon a time, there was a man who had three sons. The youngest was very good-looking, so he was called Handsome. One day, the man was going on a business trip, and he asked his three sons what they would like him to bring back for them. The first son asked for a yacht. The second son asked for a Ferrari. But the third son, Handsome, said that all he wanted was one perfect red rose.

"On his business trip, the man purchased the yacht and the Ferrari and had them sent back to the two sons. But he looked in every florist shop, and he couldn't find a perfect red rose anywhere.

"Then, on the last day of his trip, he passed a great castle. There, in the garden, he saw beautiful red roses.

He searched for the most perfect one, found it, and picked it for his youngest son.

"Suddenly, from out of the castle, came a horrible lady beast. She grabbed the man. 'You will die for stealing my rose!'

"The man pleaded, 'Oh, please, Madam Beastie, spare my life. The rose is a gift for my son.'

" 'Then you may leave, but you must send your youngest son to me in your place. And he will have to marry me. If you do not do this, I will come after you.'

"The man was horrified, but he made the promise to Madam Beastie. When he arrived home, he told his sons of his adventure. He didn't want his youngest son to leave, but Handsome was afraid that Beastie would come for his father, so he left to go to the castle.

"When Handsome saw Beastie for the first time, he was frightened. But to Handsome's surprise, Beastie behaved very nicely to him. She didn't make him marry her right away. She gave him nice things to eat, they had interesting conversations, and Handsome enjoyed being with her, even though she was very ugly and he didn't really like looking at her.

"Beastie allowed him to go away and visit his father, but when he returned, he found that Beastie was sick from missing him. He realized that he was in love with her, and he said he wanted to marry her. And suddenly there was music and fireworks and to his great surprise, he saw that Beastie had become a beautiful princess!

She'd been living under the curse of an evil witch, and not until someone of her own kind loved her could the curse be lifted.

"So Handsome married the Princess, and they lived happily ever after."

I also heard my father's version of *The Frog Prince—The Pig Princess*—a lot. My parents did everything possible to give me some kind of self-esteem. Pork chops or bacon were never served in the Wilhern household. And no one was allowed to play "this little piggy" on my toes.

There was a knock on my door.

"Miss Penelope, your four o'clock is here."

# *Chapter Five*

Mother and Wanda were waiting for me in the dining room. Jessica seemed calmer—clearly, she'd decided to change her approach.

"Penelope, darling," she crooned. "I'm very sorry I spoke so harshly to you earlier. But I'm only doing this for you, for your future, for your happiness. Penelope! Are you listening to me?"

I wasn't, but I answered, "Yes, Mother."

"Penelope, you must play your part in this. Tell me something—are you happy right now?"

At least I could answer this question honestly. "No, Mother."

"All right, then. Now, are you ready? This is an important meeting. Edward Vanderman is the most promising candidate we've ever had."

For once I didn't have to listen to Wanda recite my suitor's credentials. This was Edward's third visit, and I knew everything about him. There was no question about it—he met all the requirements to break the curse.

The Vandermans were prominent, wealthy, and most important, blue-blooded. They could trace their ancestry back to, I don't know, the Stone Age or something, and I sometimes wondered if Edward wasn't maybe a throwback to that time when brains were appreciably smaller.

He certainly hadn't retained any of the aggressive mannerisms of his ancestors. I couldn't quite imagine Edward with a club in his hand, dragging his chosen mate by her hair to his cave. He wouldn't have the guts. Not that I would ever want to be dragged around like that, by Edward or any man, but I remembered once seeing a movie where a very sexy caveman did just that.

Through the window I could see my visitor slumped in his chair. Edward—and he was the kind of person who would always be called Edward, not Ed or Eddie or any other nickname that implied familiarity, warmth, and affection—Edward was *sad*.

Okay, maybe I was being a little unkind. Physically, he wasn't horrific (and speaking as one who was, I felt qualified to make that judgment). In fact, most people would say he was a nice-looking man. He was well groomed and well dressed, and his features were normal and they were all in the right places.

It was personality that kept Edward back. I was certain that when he was a child, he was picked on by the other kids, maybe beaten up, and I wouldn't say he deserved it, but I could imagine what propelled the other little kids to gang up on him. He was a walking victim. In his opinion, nothing ever went well for him, bad things were always happening to him, and it was never his own fault.

I remembered his first visit to me. He'd started off by telling me that normally he would never respond to a matchmaking service, that he didn't have any problems finding girls, and that the only reason he'd succumbed to Wanda's invitation was that his parents thought highly of the Wilherns and had insisted he meet the Wilherns' mysterious, cursed daughter.

I responded by telling him that he'd fulfilled his obligation to his parents and mine, that clearly he could find his own mate, and that he could terminate this visit and leave right now with no hard feelings.

He fell apart completely. Suddenly he was pouring out his guts, telling me that all those girls who chased him were interested in him only because of his family's wealth and social standing, his looks, and the fact that his father owned some huge industry that Edward would ultimately inherit. He said no one knew the real Edward, that he was a prisoner of his own image, and that he'd never felt really close to anyone in his life. I was actually touched by his confession and asked him questions about himself.

"What do you like to do when you're alone, Edward?"

He replied, "I'm always alone, Penelope, even when I'm in a crowd."

"What kind of movies do you like, Edward?"

"Movies are difficult for me. Sad movies make me think about my own life. Happy movies make me even sadder because I compare them to my own life, which makes me feel even worse."

No matter what subject I brought up, he'd turn it around so it would be about him. I'd ask his opinion of national health insurance and he'd tell me about some imagined medical ailment of his own. I was losing patience.

On the other hand, he could lift the curse if he married me. As I made myself comfortable on my loveseat, my mother said, "Maybe he's not the man of your dreams, Penelope, but he'll do."

"Beggars can't be choosers," Wanda pointed out.

Jessica glared at her, but I understood what Wanda was saying. The underlying meaning was, "Don't blow this one, Penelope. He may be your best chance."

They were both right. I needed a man to save me, to release me from my curse, to give me a life. It was too much to hope that I might actually be attracted to him. I turned on the microphone.

"Hello, Edward."

I wouldn't say his face lit up at the sound of my voice, but at least there was a glimmer of expression.

"Penelope! How are you?"

How was I? How about depressed, angry, fed up with my life and the injustice of it all . . . but that wasn't what Edward wanted to hear.

"Fine, Edward. How are *you*?"

Edward obviously felt no obligation to provide the expected polite response most people made. He replied the way he always did.

"Oh, you know. Not up to par."

Edward's family belonged to a golf club, so he frequently used this term to describe the fact that he wasn't in the best spirits. I'd begun to wonder if maybe I should advise him to consider depression as his own personal par.

But I didn't. I responded in my usual sympathetic and endearing way. "I'm sorry to hear that, Edward. What's wrong?"

"I don't know where to begin."

I stifled a groan—these microphones picked up everything. "Are you having problems at work? Is your father giving you a hard time again?"

"What else is new?" Edward said glumly. "He ignores me, he never listens to my advice. Oh, Penelope, he treats me like dirt! Yesterday he bawled me out because I didn't finish some stupid report. But what could I do? It was already five o'clock, and I had to leave."

"Why did you have to leave?" I asked.

"Because it was five o'clock! I'd already put in my eight hours."

"Of course. You don't want to turn into some kind of workaholic."

"And remember I told you last time about that

scruffy little jerk he hired? The foreigner with the accent? Well, he promoted the jerk! Over me!"

I tried to sound sympathetic. "Oh, dear. Did he say why?"

"Oh, there was some nonsense about productivity. He acts like the only reason he lets me work there is because I'm his son."

Probably a good call, I thought. "How's life at home, Edward?"

"Oh, I'm treated terribly there, too. My mother is constantly nagging me to clean my room. As if we didn't have servants! And yesterday she scolded me because I came home from work for a little nap in the afternoon. She said my father doesn't let other employees have naps. Well, so what? What's the point of being a Vanderman if you can't have some privileges? But she always takes my father's side. They're both always picking on me."

His whining was beginning to grate on my nerves, but I stayed calm. "I'm sure they just want what's best for you, Edward."

"Ha!" he croaked bitterly. "I'm never good enough for them. Penelope, you have no idea what it's like to be an only child."

I didn't bother reminding him that I, too, was an only child. "Maybe you should think about moving out, getting your own place."

"I could . . . ," he said slowly. "If I found someone I could live with. Actually, I've been thinking about that a lot lately. My parents said they'd buy me a house if I settled down with a nice girl from a good family. I suppose they want grandchildren." He sighed. "Typical. They only think about themselves."

I swallowed and took a deep breath. "Do . . . do you know anyone like that, Edward? Someone you'd want to marry and settle down with?"

"Actually, that's something I wanted to talk to you about."

"Oh, really?"

"And not just because you're a Wilhern. Of course, the fact that your blood is as blue as ours would make my parents very happy. But it's much more than that. Oh, Penelope . . . you're my only friend, the only person who cares about me, the only one who listens to me. Penelope . . . I think I'm falling in love with you."

I could feel my mother and Wanda breathing down my neck.

"You understand my feelings, you can see beyond my name, my money, my good looks. You know I'm more than a rich, handsome aristocrat. And I know you must be more than your curse. You have the sensitivity to see the real me, to let me show you how sensitive I am. Let me know you, Penelope—the *real* you. Let me see beyond your curse."

"Not yet," Wanda hissed in my ear. But I wasn't so sure about that. Edward's voice had actually touched me—it was positively plaintive.

"I have this feeling, Penelope, that you're the one. No, no, that's not right, it's more, much more than simply a feeling. I *know* you're the one, my one and only. You never nag me like my mother. You wouldn't care if I took naps. You accept me just the way I am."

He moved closer to the window. "Penelope, is it at all possible that you could feel the same about me?"

"It's . . . possible," I said carefully. I had a sudden urge to touch my snout to see if it was growing.

"Penelope, *please*. I'm begging you. Come to me. Come out."

He looked so pathetic, standing there before me. He was such a nothing, an annoying nerd with no personality, a whiny little spoiled brat. A spoiled brat who had the ability to lift my curse.

I moved swiftly, before my mother or Wanda could stop me, before I could stop myself with second thoughts. I was able to get through the door before they could even cry out or react.

"Edward . . ."

He turned to me. And there it was—that look.

"Ohmigod."

"Edward?" I took a step toward him. "It's me, Penelope."

He took a step backward. "No."

"Yes."

"Nooooooooo!" he howled. He took another step backward. "Don't come any closer! Keep back! Stay away from me!" He looked around frantically. "Somebody, help me! Help me!"

"Edward, stop it. I'm not going to hurt you," I said, but without thinking I took another step toward him while I spoke. Edward went over the edge. I could still hear the echo of his screams long after he'd fled the room.

# Chapter Six

"How ya doing, Lemon?"

"Not bad," the reporter replied. While his one good eye adjusted to the harsh fluorescent lighting of the police station, he fiddled with the patch over the other eye. There'd been a time when he'd hoped that the unfortunate loss of his eye would lead to a cool pirate nickname—Captain Hook, Jack Sparrow, something like that. But it wasn't to be. After twenty-five years, he had come to accept that he would always be known by his last name, the name endowed by his family— *Lemon.* Like a used car that turned out to be worthless. *Lemon,* synonymous with *loser.* Which made sense, since, after a quarter of a century, he was still a nobody reporter on the same old beat.

"Anything happening, Al?" he asked the sergeant at the desk.

"Not much. Four-car pileup on the highway. Break-in on Eighty-fourth Street. A brawl behind the Madison."

Lemon perked up. The Madison was a pretty upscale hotel. "Any celebrities involved?"

"Nah."

The door to the station burst open, and a distraught man burst in. "Help! I need help!" He looked over his shoulder fearfully. "Is she behind me?"

"Something wrong, sir?" the sergeant asked.

"I've been attacked!"

"Yes, sir. Who attacked you?"

"Not who, *what*! A creature, a monster! You have to go after her, arrest her, lock her up!"

A couple of cops snickered, and the sergeant behind the desk rolled his eyes. "Yes, sir, a monster attacked you, that's just terrible. Hey, Joe, we got space in the tank for him to sleep it off?"

"I am not drunk!" the man declared indignantly.

"Just calm down, sir."

"Do you know who I am?"

"No, sir, I'm afraid I don't."

But Lemon did. He'd suddenly recognized the face from his newspaper's society page. "You're Vanderman's son, aren't you?"

"I am Edward Vanderman Junior, yes. And I'm telling you that a monster has attacked me."

The sergeant groaned, but he took out a form and wrote down the victim's name. "Can you be more specific, Mr. Vanderman? What kind of monster was it?"

"Haven't you been listening to me?" Edward cried. "Not *it, she!*"

"Ah, a female monster. Four arms, eight legs?"

Edward shook his head fiercely. "No, no . . ."

"The head of a dragon?"

"No, not a dragon. A pig."

Lemon drew in his breath sharply. "You saw a woman who looked like a pig?"

"Oh, yeah, I think I know her," one of the cops said. "Sounds like the beast my brother-in-law fixed me up with last week." The guys cracked up, but Lemon didn't join in. This wasn't just the son of a tycoon having a nervous breakdown. He had a gut feeling there was a bigger story here.

Edward threw himself across the sergeant's desk. "Don't let them laugh at me! I know what I saw! She had the face of a pig. With fangs!"

"Okay, fellow, just calm down. Take a deep breath." Out of the corner of his mouth, the sergeant muttered, "Get some cuffs."

Lemon stepped forward. "That won't be necessary, Al. He's with me." He thrust an arm through Vanderman's. "Come with me, Edward. I want to hear all about your pig-lady."

# Chapter Seven

Mass hysteria had taken over the Wilhern household. My mother was sobbing buckets of tears and wailing at the top of her lungs while my father tried to comfort her. Wanda was screaming at Jake.

"What do you *mean* you couldn't catch him?"

Jake, in true butler fashion, remained calm. "I'm terribly sorry, madam, but I didn't expect him to react so dramatically. And he moved with extraordinary speed. I ran as fast as I could, but by the time I'd reached the front gates, he had disappeared."

"I could call the police," my father offered. "They could put out an all points bulletin."

"Franklin, he didn't commit a *crime*!" my mother shrieked. "You can't have a man arrested because he didn't sign a gag order!" She paced the room. "We're finished, finished! The word will be all over town by tomorrow. We'll have to change our names, move away, *far* away." She stopped to glare at me. "And you,

Penelope, why, why, *why* did you reveal yourself like that? It was too soon!"

"Mother, what else could I do? He was begging me to come out."

"You could have put him off."

"For how long? He was already saying he loved me. Eventually he'd have to *see* me. I don't think putting it off would have made any difference."

"Well, we'll never know now, will we?" my mother fumed. "I wonder if we should raise your dowry. Maybe that would tempt Edward back."

"Jessica, the Vandermans are wealthy," my father pointed out. "Just as all the people like us are. A larger dowry wouldn't influence them."

I couldn't take any more of this madness. "If you will all excuse me, I'm going to the solarium," I announced, and no one tried to stop me.

But I found no comfort in the solarium. Even my plants looked sad and hopeless. The sun was setting, so I turned on the fake-sun lights. Unfortunately, I was then able to catch a glimpse of my reflection in the shadows on the glass. If there was anything uglier than a pig-faced girl, it was a pig-faced girl crying.

An awful memory came rushing back. I couldn't have been more than six or seven, and I'd wandered into a guest bedroom for some reason. From the window, I had a view I'd never had before. It must have been some sort of school playground—I could see children playing, running around, tossing balls back and forth.

It was the first time I'd ever seen real, live children my own age. For a while, I just watched in awe and amazement. Occasionally, the echo of a giggle or a squeal would reach my ears.

I'd never had any other children around me, and I wanted to play with them. Hurrying out of the room, I went down the back stairs of the house. I wasn't even trying to hide myself, but nobody saw me as I ran through a warren of rooms and out a door. Following the sound of the voices, I circled the house. The mansion was surrounded by gates and hedges, but I was able to pinpoint the place where, just yards away and blocked from view, the children were playing.

I couldn't reach them, of course, or even see them through the barriers. But then, miracle of miracles, a ball came flying over the gate. I heard the kids yelling, and I wondered if I should yell back. I didn't need to. Apparently, a couple of them were good climbers. Two heads appeared at the top of the hedge.

"Hey, girl, can you throw back our ball?" one of them called. I looked up.

The screams of the two kids brought other kids climbing up the gate to see me. Half were screaming, half were laughing. Their cries drew out my mother and Jake. The next thing I knew, I was being scooped up by my mother while Jake chased off the children. I never knew if they got their ball back.

I had cried that day. "Why did they laugh at me, Mommy?" I'd asked. "Why were they afraid of me? Was it my face?"

"That's not your face," my mother said over and over. "It's the curse. Someday you'll have your real face, and no one will scream when they see you."

But eventually I reached my teens, I still didn't have my real face, and that's when I started crying on pretty much a full-time basis.

# Chapter Eight

Books. I had lots of books. They were my best friends and my worst enemies.

Until I was twelve or thirteen, reading was a pleasure. I moved from fairy tales to fantasies, stories with dragons and trolls, myths, science fiction, alien worlds. It was all pretend, which suited me just fine. It was better than having to rely on my own imagination all the time for entertainment.

But then I discovered books that had to do with real life. Biographies, books about travel, memoirs, and journals. Fiction, too, novels that didn't involve magic or intergalactic space battles but that took place in the real world, with characters my age who did things, who went to high school and played sports, who had friends, who fell in love. That's when I realized what I was missing. And that's when I got really mad. If a typical teenager could feel that life was unjust because her boobs were small, imagine how I felt.

I wanted to hang out at malls, go to dances, try out

for cheerleading. All I could do was read about life. I couldn't *live* it.

I tried hobbies. I took up painting, pottery, knitting. I had piano lessons (a major coup for my parents, who located a blind piano teacher). But I had to do all of these things alone, and I got bored with them. I played chess with my father, which I actually liked, but not enough to play six hours a day. I wasn't a nerd, for crying out loud.

My father was very anti-television, so I hadn't been exposed to much of that, but by the time I was fifteen I was complaining so much about my deprived life that he broke down and put one in my bedroom. My general state of mind went from bad to worse.

Teens on TV had it all—they were beautiful, they went to the beach, they had dramatic love affairs. Of course, I didn't know then that there was more fantasy in that teen TV world than there'd been in my fairy tales. For me, the TV shows didn't just provide entertainment, they confirmed the injustice of my world and gave me more excuses to cry.

Ultimately, I discovered video games, Nintendo, and PlayStation, which kept me amused for some time. Then there were chat rooms and virtual reality Web sites, where I could reinvent myself and have something that remotely resembled communication with other people. I took to writing bad dark poetry in a feeble imitation of Sylvia Plath, and I became an expert at giving myself home manicures.

And somehow I made it to the age of eighteen. That was when my mother had hired Wanda, from a professional matchmaking agency, to assist her in the task to which she could now devote herself: finding Prince Charming, who would fall in love with me so deeply that he could accept my face and marry me so the curse would be lifted.

Life with me couldn't have been easy for my parents. It wasn't easy for any of us, living in a fairy tale with no happy ending in sight, when there was a real world out there somewhere that we couldn't touch. And here I was now, at the age of twenty-five; people were still running away from me, and I was still crying.

Stop it, I ordered myself. Edward Vanderman is not worth your tears. You didn't even like him!

But maybe that was why I was crying. Because there remained that one horrible fact: If a pathetic creature like Edward Vanderman, who was desperate to get married, ran away from me in horror—who wouldn't? I wondered if maybe it wouldn't be best to give up right now, and—and do what? Kill myself? No, it would break my poor father's heart and he'd be overcome with guilt.

Besides, I didn't want to die. I wanted to *live*. Not like this, hidden away, all alone. I wanted to live like real people, normal people. The people I read about, the characters I saw on TV—okay, maybe not *them*, since I didn't have any real interest in playing beach volleyball or developing an eating disorder. I just wanted to be *out*.

"Penelope, my child."

I wiped my eyes quickly before my father could see the tears. "Hi, Dad."

"I'm so very, very sorry."

"It's not your fault that Edward Vanderman ran away," I said. "You're not responsible."

"No, you know what I mean, my dear. In the long run, it's all my fault. It was my family that gave you this—this problem."

I turned back to my reflection and put a hand over my "problem." Funny how I almost looked human. Then I caught a glimpse of my father's face behind me. He was in as much pain as I was, and I felt even sadder for him than I felt for myself.

I went to him and kissed his cheek. "It's going to be okay, Dad," I said, and tried to sound like I really believed this. Then my mother and Wanda came running into the solarium with Jake bringing up the rear. The women were squealing about some brilliant new idea, and I pretended for my father's sake to be interested.

"I can't believe we didn't think of this sooner!" my mother exclaimed.

"What's your idea?" I asked.

Wanda turned to my father. "This curse—there was no mention of nationality, was there?"

He looked at her blankly. "Huh?"

"Prince Charming, the man who can lift the curse. I know he has to be one of your own kind, but that just means a blue blood, right? He doesn't have to be from around here, does he?"

My father's brow furrowed. "No, I don't think so. Why?"

My mother spoke up. "Because all this time we've been trying to find an aristocrat among our own local set! Why not a foreign one?"

"A foreign aristocrat?" he asked. "How would he be any different from an American one?"

"Other nationalities have different standards of beauty," Wanda stated. "I've heard of a tribe in South America where the fatter a woman is, the more beautiful she's considered to be."

"Penelope is not fat!" my mother declared indignantly.

"That's just an example," Wanda said. "All I'm saying is that beauty is in the eye of the beholder, and some nationalities behold people differently from others."

"Is there a nationality that appreciates pig faces?" I asked doubtfully.

"That's not the point," Wanda said briskly. "I'm simply saying that we need to extend our search criteria."

"There's something else, too," my mother declared eagerly. "Europe is full of decayed aristocracy. People with titles and castles but no money. A significant dowry could be very appealing to them."

"Oh, dear. Does this mean we have to move to Europe?" my father asked.

"That won't be necessary," Wanda assured him. "Haven't you ever heard of Eurotrash? The city is filled with ex-pat Europeans! They come here for temporary jobs but then they want to stay."

My mother picked up the narrative. "Which they can't, because they need passports or visas or green cards or something."

Wanda finished it off. "And what's the easiest way to get a permanent residency? Marriage!"

My mother rubbed her hands together gleefully. "We have to get to work on our database. There's a whole world of foreign Prince Charmings out there and we have to identify them. Come along, Franklin. We need all the help we can get and there's no time to lose."

With one last apologetic look shot in my direction, he followed them out. Only Jake remained behind.

"Would you like your tea in here, Miss Penelope?"

"Yes, okay, thank you, Jake. Jake! Wait."

"Yes, miss?"

I gazed at the butler thoughtfully. "What do *you* think of that idea?"

"It's not my place to have an opinion on the matter, Miss Penelope."

I sighed. "Well, you want to know what *I* think? I don't think it's going to make one bit of difference where the guys come from. They're still going to run away. Only they'll be screaming in French or Spanish or Italian."

I could have sworn I saw a glimmer of sympathy behind those reserved eyes. But all he said was, "I wouldn't
know, miss."

I folded my arms across my chest. "I'm going to
cooperate, Jake. I'm going to meet their decayed aristocracy. But Jake, please see me before making any
appointments. I want to arrange the meetings."

"As you wish, miss," he said, and left the solarium.

As I wish. As *if.*

# Chapter Nine

"This is what I don't understand, Edward," Lemon said as they sat down in the bar. There were only a few people there, and the TV set was turned up loud to the local news. They could talk without being overheard or interrupted.

"You knew about the curse. Why were you so shocked when you saw Penelope?"

"When I heard that she was a pig-girl, I thought that meant she was a little chubby," Edward replied. "I could have dealt with that. But I'm telling you, she's a monster!" He looked at Lemon curiously. "How come you believed me when the police didn't?"

"You see this patch?" Lemon asked. "It indicates the lack of an eye. I lost the eye when I was following up a rumor about a baby with the face of a pig. It's about time I got some compensation. Not to mention revenge on that— that—" He shuddered, unable to get the word out.

"Monster pig-girl?" Edward offered.

"No. Her mother. I still have nightmares about that

woman coming after me with that soup ladle. They tried to make me believe that the baby was dead, but I knew they were bluffing. I've been waiting twenty-five years to get some proof of Penelope's existence."

"Well, I'm telling you right now, she exists," Edward declared. Then, suddenly, his face went pasty white. He stared at the TV screen. "What the hell . . . ?"

Lemon turned to see what had grabbed Edward's attention. It was Edward's own face. On the television.

"I've been attacked! Do something! There's a monster out there!"

The camera shifted to the face of a reporter in a newsroom setting. "That was Edward Vanderman Junior, son of Edward Vanderman, CEO of Vanderman Industries, who appears to have had a nervous breakdown today. Details coming up on the six o'clock report."

Edward buried his face in his hands. "Ohmigod, ohmigod. Where did that come from?"

"Surveillance camera," Lemon said. "They're in all the police stations."

Edward's cell phone rang. He stared at it fearfully, and then picked it up.

"Hello? Yes, Father. I know, Father. Of course not, Father! I'm coming back to the office now. Really?" He gulped, put a hand over the phone's mouthpiece, and spoke to Lemon. "My father says the building is surrounded by the media. They want details about my nervous breakdown." He spoke into the phone again. "Then

I'll go home. What? All right, Father. Yes, yes, I'll do something about it! Good-bye."

He turned the phone off. "They've surrounded our house, too! My mother is going to have a real nervous breakdown. What am I going to do?"

He looked so pathetic and helpless that Lemon took pity. "You're going to help me expose the truth about Penelope. I'll even give you credit in the story. Then everyone will know that you were telling the truth, that you weren't hallucinating or having a nervous breakdown."

Edward absorbed this and calmed down. "Yes. Yes, that could work, that could save my reputation. I'm your witness, I actually saw her. And wait till my father finds out what I've uncovered about the Wilherns. I just might impress him for a change."

"I need more than a witness for the story, Edward," Lemon said. "I need a photo."

Edward went very still. "A photo?"

"A picture of Penelope. Real, tangible proof that I can publish with my story. Do you think you can get back into the Wilhern mansion?"

Edward had gone so pale Lemon was afraid he'd pass out right there at the bar. "You're not serious!" he whimpered. "You want me to take a picture of her? There's no way I'm going back into that house." His voice was rising. "I never want to see that face again. I can't! I can't!"

Geez, what a jerk. It was all Lemon could do to

refrain from slapping him. "Calm down, calm down." The guy was a serious wimp, but he was Lemon's only connection. "We'll find someone else to go and meet her. My paper will put up a bribe, maybe five thousand."

"You'll need more than money to find someone whom the matchmaking agency will approve," Edward said. "Don't forget, any man who wants to meet her has to be an aristocrat, a real blue blood. I don't know any blue bloods who are desperate for money."

He had a point. Lemon considered the dilemma. Then he recalled something—a minor bit that had appeared in his paper's gossip column recently. He smiled.

"Wait a minute. I think I do."

# Chapter Ten

*Parallel Penelope: A Fantasy of Real Life*
*by Penelope Wilhern*

When Jessica Wilhern was giving birth to her baby, she and her husband, Franklin Wilhern, were a little nervous. Legend had it that a curse had been placed by a witch on the Wilhern family one hundred fifty years earlier when Ralph Wilhern had refused to marry the witch's daughter and the daughter committed suicide. The witch declared that the next daughter born to the Wilherns would have the face of a pig.

Jessica did give birth to a daughter. But since all that business about a curse was nonsense and there were no such things as witches anyway, the child was absolutely perfect and bore absolutely no resemblance whatsoever to a pig. And they named her Penelope.

The family was filled with joy. Little Penelope was a delight from the day she was born, and she never gave her parents a moment of worry. The Wilherns, a wealthy and socially prominent family, gave their daughter a privileged life. She went to a private school, she had extravagant birthday parties, and on every vacation she went with her parents to exotic places like Egypt and India and China where she met fascinating people and had exciting experiences. Her mother and father liked to show her off to people because they were so proud of her.

As she grew up, she became prettier and prettier, and by the age of sixteen she was beautiful. She was also very nice and very smart, and she became the most popular girl in her high school. She was head cheerleader, she played on the basketball team, she was Juliet in the school production of *Romeo and* . . .

In her senior year, she was elected student body president and prom queen. She had fifteen best friends, hundreds of regular friends, and a different boyfriend every month. Her hobby was figure skating and she just skated for fun, but she was so good that she was invited to join the Olympic team, gave a flawless performance, and won the gold medal.

She made her debut at a grand ball, and all the newspapers called her the debutante of the year. Her picture was in all the magazines, and she became legendary for her poise, her charm, and, of course, her beauty.

Of course, all the finest men in the world wanted to marry her. Famous men, brilliant men, men who were so handsome they took her breath away came begging for dates. She went out with them, and sometimes she let them kiss her, and every single one of them asked her to marry him. But she always said no, thank you. Penelope was waiting for someone very, very special. Someone not just handsome, not just smart and rich and famous. He had to be special in a special way.

One day, there was a knock on her door. A man stood there, but he was not an ordinary man. There was something very special about him. He had rabbit ears. Two great pink rabbit ears instead of regular normal ears.

People laughed at him and made fun of him, and some people were afraid of him because he looked so different. But Penelope was smarter than most people. She could see deep into the rabbit man, and she knew he was the perfect man for her.

Rabbit Man asked her to marry him, and Penelope said yes. All her friends thought she was crazy, because she could have any man in the whole wide world. But Penelope wanted Rabbit Man because she knew he was the best man in the whole wide world.

They had a great big wedding. And when they were pronounced husband and wife, she kissed him, and something amazing happened. He turned into Prince Charming. He told her that a wicked witch had put a spell on him, and it could only be lifted when a girl fell in love with him just as he was.

Prince Charming took Penelope to his golden castle. They had lots of children and the most biggest garden in the universe. Now, you probably think the next line will be "and they lived happily ever after." But this is not the end of the story. Because Penelope made an amazing discovery.

There were many girls in the world who were not as beautiful as she was, and some of them were downright ugly. She met girls who had donkey ears and fish mouths and frog eyes, and even girls who had pig snouts instead of noses.

Penelope wanted to help these poor girls who weren't born as fortunate as she was. So she decided to become a doctor and devote her life to fixing girls with animal parts. All the ugly girls became beautiful girls, they all found handsome boyfriends, and everyone lived happily ever after.

The End

Okay, I was only ten when I wrote it. But at least it proves that I wasn't completely self-centered.

# Chapter Eleven

"You ever heard of Max Campion?" Lemon asked as they walked to the Cloverdilly Pub.

"The real estate Campions? I know the name. Max Campion. No, never met him."

"I never met the guy but I've heard plenty," Lemon said. "His old man was Clarence Campion, the real estate mogul. He died a couple of years ago and left Max his fortune. And Max blew the whole wad gambling."

"And you think he can help us out?"

"The guy's got it all," Lemon told him. "*Social Register,* old family, all that crap. But he's completely broke. Rumor has it he's been passing bad checks. My contact says we can find him at the Cloverdilly. He's a regular in their back gambling room."

The Cloverdilly had just started filling up with the after-work crowd. Behind the bar, the bartender was slamming the brews down in front of customers and the jukebox was blasting old rhythm and blues. Lemon, with Edward at his side, moved through the room to a doorway leading to another, smaller room. A beefy-looking man hopped off a stool and stopped them.

"Whattaya want?"

"We're looking for Max Campion," Lemon said.

The man's eyes narrowed. "Why?"

"Got a little proposition to make him."

The bouncer or whatever he was looked them up and down, and must have decided they didn't look like cops or gangsters. He jerked his chin in the direction of a table, where a heavyset guy, a blue-haired woman, an old man, and a younger one were playing cards.

"That's him."

The younger guy with shaggy hair was getting up. "I'm out," he muttered, and he tossed his cards on the table. With his hands in the pockets of his battered leather jacket and his head down, he brushed past Lemon and Edward. They followed him through the bar and out onto the street.

"Hey, Campion," Lemon called.

The guy kept moving.

"Come on, fellow, wait up!"

The young guy looked over his shoulder. "What do you want?"

"Listen, Campion, I got a proposition for you."

Campion scowled. "You got the wrong guy."

"You haven't heard the proposition," Lemon said. "Interested in making an easy five grand?"

Campion actually stopped. Now that Lemon could

get a good look at him, he could see that the guy was younger than he thought he'd be. He looked pretty worn out, though, like someone who had been gambling all night long. For many nights. And losing.

He gave them a tired, crooked grin. "Who do I have to kill?"

"Nothing like that, man. All you got to do is pretend you're interested in Penelope Wilhern, take a photo of her, and give it to me."

"I don't have a camera."

"I'll lend you a camera."

"Why don't you hire some paparazzi guy?"

"Because a paparazzi guy wouldn't be able to get into the Wilhern house," Edward told him. "The only men who can meet Penelope are people like us. Not like him." He indicated Lemon. "Like you and me."

"You and me," Campion repeated. "What do we have in common?"

"I'm a Vanderman. You're a Campion."

"So?"

"We're aristocrats."

Campion started laughing. "Yeah? Well, I must be the one and only aristocrat who's completely broke."

"Exactly!" Lemon said. "That's why we figured maybe you'd take the job. You got the credentials and you need the money."

Campion considered this. "And who's this Penelope Wilhern? Another aristocrat?"

"You never heard of the pig-girl?" Edward asked. "People think she's a myth, but I'm telling you, she's absolutely real. And I'm warning you, she could be dangerous. Just be prepared."

Campion's lips twitched. "I think I can handle myself with a girl. Even a pig-girl."

"Excellent!" Lemon declared happily. "Let's talk."

# Chapter Twelve

"I like the sound of this one," my mother said. "Dietrich von Strudelhoffer. Take a look at his picture, Penelope."

I took a quick glance at the very blond, bare-chested hunk in the photo. "I dunno. He's okay, I guess. Looks like a bodybuilder."

"He's *Baron* Dietrich von Strudelhoffer," Wanda pointed out. "Very old title, Middle Ages or something. You'd be a baroness, Penelope. There's a duke around here somewhere, too."

We were sitting around the dining room table, going over the men I'd be meeting today. "Is there anyone from France?" I asked.

Wanda rummaged through a few folders and opened one. "Henri de Villeneuve. No title, but the 'de' means he's an aristocrat."

I checked out the photo. "Kind of old."

"There's nothing in the curse about the age of your

Prince Charming. And he has a château, Penelope. It needs some work, but . . ."

My mother clapped her hands. "Ooh, a fixer-upper! What fun!" She beamed at me. "Wouldn't you love to renovate a château, darling?"

"Sure," I said. "I'd love it."

"I'm so happy you're getting into this new direction, Penelope. Aren't you excited about meeting all these foreigners?"

"Absolutely," I said.

My mother was clearly pleased that I wasn't responding with my usual sarcasm, and she didn't appear to be at all surprised by my new ardor. Wanda, however, was looking at me with downright suspicion.

Actually, I *was* a little excited, or maybe it was just nerves. I'd never done anything quite like this before. I was determined that nothing would go wrong today.

"I'm going to go check on your father, darling. And you should be getting ready. What time is your first visitor coming?"

"Ten o'clock," I said. "Pierre, I think. Or maybe it's Enrique. I can't remember."

"I still don't understand why you insisted on making the arrangements yourself," my mother said. "That's what I pay Wanda to do."

I shrugged. "I just wanted to get more involved in the whole thing."

My mother looked so happy to hear this I almost felt

guilty. "Fourteen interviews! It's going to be a very long day for you, Penelope."

"I'll manage," I said.

My mother left the room, and Wanda looked at me quizzically. I sensed that she was on the verge of interrogating me about this sudden interest I was showing, but then her cell phone rang.

"Yes, Wanda here." She frowned. "No, we're only seeing foreigners today. And we've already got fourteen interviews lined up." Her frown deepened. "Just a minute, I'll ask her." She turned to me. "The agency's just heard from an American who wants to be seen today. Can you squeeze him in? I know you've got a full schedule."

"Sure," I said. "He can come at ten."

"I thought you just said you were seeing someone else at ten."

"I meant ten thirty."

Her eyes narrowed, but she returned to her phone call. "All right, he can come at ten. What's the name?" She hung up. "He's Maxwell Campion."

"Okay."

"Don't you want to write that down?"

"I'll remember," I said.

She looked at me warily. Wanda could be a lot more astute about me than my mother, who only saw what she wanted to see. I needed to allay Wanda's qualms about my new zeal.

"How did you get into this business, Wanda?" I asked. "I mean, it's an interesting line of work, matchmaking. How do you train for it?"

Wanda countered with her own question. "What's your sudden interest?" she asked. "I've been working here seven years and you've never asked me about myself before."

"Just curious," I said lightly. "Who knows, maybe once I have my real face, I might want to get into some kind of career."

"Not matchmaking," Wanda said flatly. "You have to have a calling."

"You mean, like a nun?"

"Yes. You have to have a very strong belief."

"In what?" I asked. "Love? Marriage?"

"You have to believe that there's someone for everyone. That each person in the world has a soul mate that he or she is meant to be with."

"I don't need a soul mate," I stated. "Just someone who won't run away screaming when he sees me."

"You have been my greatest challenge," Wanda acknowledged.

"But you're bound and determined to succeed, right?"

"I'm trying, Penelope," she said.

"Only there's one thing I don't get," I remarked. "If I've got a soul mate out there, why do you keep pushing me to marry anyone who can lift the curse?"

She smiled, a little sadly. "Just because he's out there, Penelope, doesn't mean you'll ever find him."

Through the window into the music room, I saw Jake, and I switched on the microphone system.

"I'll be ready at ten, Jake."

"Very good, Miss Penelope."

I then went to my room, to change my clothes and brush my hair. My mother liked me to do this before interviews. Even though I wouldn't be seen, she thought I'd come across as more appealing if I looked as good as possible. Today, for once, I wasn't going to argue with her.

When I returned to the dining room just before ten, she was already there with Wanda, and telling Jake to bring in some sandwiches at lunchtime so we wouldn't have to take a break from interviews. Jake looked at me with raised eyebrows. I just shrugged.

"Are you ready, Miss Penelope?"

"Yes, Jake." He left the dining room. A moment later, he entered the music room and stood by the open door. A middle-aged, elegant-looking gray-haired man in a fashionable blue suit entered.

Behind me, my mother and Wanda were stationed at each shoulder. "Ooh, he's distinguished," Jessica said. "Not very tall, but he has excellent posture. Is that the Frenchman with the château?"

"No, I believe he's the Swiss banker."

"Well, I think he looks nice," my mother noted.

"Yes," Wanda agreed. And then she said, "So does he."

Another man entered the room—the tall, blond German with the muscular build. He was followed by a swarthy, mustached man wearing something black and Italian, and then a seriously tanned fellow with an open shirt revealing a multitude of chains came in.

"Penelope!" my mother exclaimed. "I don't understand. What's going on?"

I clamped my hand over the microphone. "I'm interviewing them all together, Mother."

"But this is ridiculous, Penelope! Why in the world would you want to do that?"

"Because I want to get it all over with."

Wanda threw up her hands in despair while my mother shrieked, "Franklin! Get in here right this minute and talk some sense into your daughter!"

Calmly, I turned back to the window. The room was filling up now, and I gauged the expressions of the candidates. A few of them looked confident, even cocky, others were clearly uncomfortable, and a couple of them looked very nervous. I heard several languages, and I wondered if they were talking about me. And how much they'd heard about me. Not that it mattered. Most of them probably didn't want a wife; they wanted green cards.

In accordance with my instructions, Jake brought in trays of coffee and bagels. The event was taking on the appearance of a brunch, and I decided it was time to get the show on the road.

My father entered the dining room, and my mother frantically began explaining what I'd done. I put a finger to my lips, and she rolled her eyes, but she stopped talking as I turned on the microphone.

I was about to begin speaking when a latecomer appeared. I wasn't sure why he drew my attention—maybe because, unlike the others, he looked neither cocky nor nervous. He looked . . . tired.

His shaggy hair was in need of a cut, and it was tousled in that just-woke-up way. There were deep, dark circles under his eyes. While the others were in suits, he wore jeans. At least he wore a jacket and tie with the jeans, but the jacket was too big for him, and the tie didn't go with his shirt. While the other men varied in appearance, they were all well groomed. This guy looked scruffy.

But cute. Very cute. So cute that I couldn't take my eyes off him.

No one else paid attention to him as he moved across the room. Then he did something else that was odd—while the others had remained standing, he sat down in the one comfortable chair and closed his eyes. He was certainly relaxed, I thought.

It was time to begin. And then, suddenly, for no reason that I could identify, I made a new decision. I turned off the microphone and stood up.

"I've changed my mind," I announced to my parents and Wanda.

"Thank goodness," my mother said, and Wanda looked relieved, too.

"I'll go in and make separate appointments with each of them," she said, and started toward the door.

But I moved faster, too quickly for anyone to stop me, and disregarded my mother's cry of protest as I crossed the room and opened the door to the music room.

"Good morning, gentlemen. I'm Penelope."

I was greeted pretty much as I'd expected, with a dead silence. The expressions ran the gamut, from shock to terror. The response times varied, but within seconds there was a crush at the other door as they all tried to get out of the room at the same time. I turned and went back out the way I'd come in.

My mother was sobbing, her face buried in her hands. My father, as usual, was patting her shoulder. Wanda was clutching her head, massaging her temples as if she had a massive headache.

"Why, Penelope?" my mother was moaning. "Why, why, why?"

"Like I told you, Mother, I wanted to get it over with. What was the point of dragging it out? They were all going to run, sooner or later."

Wanda was looking out the window. "Someone didn't run."

I joined her there. Sure enough, the cute, scruffy guy was still in the armchair, and now he was gazing around curiously. As I watched, he rose and began exploring the room. First, he picked up a china figurine, examined it, and then put it back down. An ashtray briefly attracted his attention next, and then he looked at a silver candy dish, turning it over in his hands before putting it down.

He made his way over to the ornate bookcase and perused the shelves. He seemed to select a book at random, and I was intrigued, because it was a book I recognized by its cover. He opened it and turned a couple of pages. He looked to the left, and to the right. And then he slipped the book inside his jacket.

I turned on the mike. "Are you interested in the work of George Rockham?"

He didn't appear to be startled by the sound of my voice. In fact, he looked directly at me—well, not really at me, but that's how it felt. I shivered, even though I knew he was actually looking into the mirror that made up the other side of the window.

"Aha!" he said. "So that's it. A one-way mirror. Like the ones they use for police lineups."

"And are you so very familiar with police lineups?" I asked.

He had the courtesy to look abashed. "No. All evidence to the contrary."

"You didn't answer my question. Do you like George Rockham?"

"Who's George Rockham?"

"The author of the book you just stole," I said. "Look, I know it's an autographed first edition, but it's not worth all that much. You could do a lot better."

He took the book out of his jacket and put it down on the table. "So, this one's not valuable."

"Not really. If you're looking for something that's worth big bucks, there's a first edition of *Moby Dick* on the third shelf."

"*Moby Dick,* huh? But *this* one," and he nodded at the one he'd taken earlier, "this is your favorite."

I was taken aback. "How did you know?"

He just grinned. I looked at Wanda's list of candidates. Since this guy didn't have any kind of foreign accent, I was able to hazard a guess at his identity.

"You must be Max Campion."

"I must be."

He was still smiling. I liked his smile. Then he yawned.

"Tired?" I asked.

"Yeah, kind of. I was up late."

"So you're a party animal."

"Oh yeah, absolutely," he said in a way that made it clear he wasn't.

"Well . . . maybe you need to go home and get some sleep."

He nodded. "Sounds like a good idea."

And then, impulsively, I asked, "Do you want to come back tomorrow?"

He cocked his head to one side, and looked at me— into the mirror—thoughtfully. "Yeah. Okay."

Then he was gone.

I'd forgotten anyone else was with me in the dining room until I heard my mother murmur in awe, "Ohmigod."

"Why didn't he run?" I wondered out loud. "He must have seen me when I went into the music room. Wanda, didn't he see me?"

"I don't know," Wanda said, and there was wonderment in her voice, too. "I presume so. Unless he's blind."

I got up and went into the music room. The book he'd tossed on the table was still there, and I picked it up. My father came into the room. "What have you got there?" he asked.

"The book that guy took off the shelf. *The Magic Inside,* by George Rockham. The story about the invisible princess. You gave it to me when I was twelve, remember?"

"I remember," he said. "You loved that book. You read it over and over."

"I felt like I could have been the princess," I said, "the way no one could see the real her. I carried this book around with me." And when I opened it, I saw a confirmation of that. In my twelve-year-old handwriting, I'd written: "Property of Penelope Wilhern. This is my favorite book." I shook my head ruefully. "So that's how he knew."

"But even so," my father said, waving a hand at the bookcase. "From all those books, he chose that one. Maybe it's an omen."

"I don't believe in omens," I said. But deep in my stomach, or somewhere else inside, I felt something. A strange little flutter, a thrill, something totally unfamiliar, and yet . . . I thought maybe I knew what it meant.

# Chapter Thirteen

❧ ～ ❧

Lemon maneuvered the van into the same space he'd used the day before. He turned around and faced Max.

"Are you ready? Is the camera working?"

"Yeah, yeah."

"Show me."

Max lifted his left arm. Nothing happened.

"It's under your *right* arm," Lemon reminded him.

"Oh, okay." Raising his right arm, a little *click* sound was barely audible.

Edward spoke nervously. "Are you sure you're going to remember that? I still can't believe you didn't get a shot of her yesterday."

"Slipped my mind," Max muttered.

"You took long enough *not* taking a picture," Lemon grumbled.

"Yeah," Edward said. "When all those other guys came running out, I thought you'd be with them. How could you stay in the same room with her all that time? Weren't you freaking out, seeing her for the first time?" He shuddered at his own memory. "She's grotesque."

"I don't scare easily," Max said. "Look, I wouldn't have been able to get a good shot of her yesterday anyway. There were too many people. Today, it's just going to be me and her."

Lemon frowned. "Couldn't you at least have shaved for the girl?" He handed him the same tie and jacket he'd lent Max the day before. "You look like hell," he commented. "Were you up all night again?"

"I'll bet he blew the whole five grand at the card table," Edward said.

"What do you care?" Max asked. "I don't look any worse today than I looked yesterday. And she invited me back, didn't she?"

"Of course she invited you back," Edward said. "She's desperate."

"You can't stay too long," Lemon warned him. "I'm worried someone from the house might look out and see me." He shuddered. "I don't want that mother coming at me again. I need the one eye I've got left."

Max nodded. "Yeah, okay."

"Besides," Lemon said, "it's not like you want to lead the poor girl on and make her think you really care. No point in hurting her. She hasn't hurt anyone."

"She tried!" Edward yelped. "I told you, she attacked me!"

"Yeah, yeah, whatever. Just get the photo, Campion, okay?"

"I will." Max got out of the van and started up the walkway to the Wilhern house.

# Chapter Fourteen

I felt like I'd been holding my breath all morning. Would he really come back? And if he did . . . why? Maybe he was just being nice. Maybe he felt sorry for me.

I was alone today. I'd barred my parents and Wanda from the dining room, hoping that might take the edge off the weirdness of it all. Jake came into the music room and spoke in my direction.

"Miss Penelope, you have a visitor."

I turned on the microphone. "Testing, testing, one, two, three."

Jake nodded. "It's working. Shall I show the gentleman in, miss?"

"Yes, please. Thank you, Jake."

Jake left, and returned a moment later with Max. "Mr. Maxwell Campion, Miss Penelope." He left, and Max looked at the mirror.

"Hi."

For some reason I didn't say anything.

"Are you there?" he asked. After a few seconds, he shrugged and ambled over to the bookcase like he'd done the day before. "Now, let's see, where was that first edition of *Moby Dick*?" he asked aloud. I remained silent.

After he examined the shelves for a while, he moved over to the piano. He stood there, gazing at it for some time before he lifted the lid to expose the keys. With one hand, he picked out a few notes.

"Do you play?" I asked.

He whirled around and grinned. "I knew you were there all this time."

"How?" I asked. "Could you hear me breathing?"

"No. I just . . . knew."

That fluttery feeling was coursing through me again. Had he just sort of sensed my presence? I tried very hard to suppress any response that might sound sentimental, and spoke matter-of-factly.

"You could play something if you like."

He shut the lid. "No, thanks."

"But you *do* play the piano," I said.

"Used to. What about you? You play any musical instruments?"

"My parents made me take piano lessons when I was a little girl," I told him. "But I didn't have any musical talent and I got tired of it."

"I'll bet you've got *some* kind of talent," he said.

"I'm good with plants," I admitted.

"Yeah? You got a big garden?"

"It's a conservatory," I said. "Indoors."

He nodded. "I guess it's too cold out right now to do any gardening."

Did he really think it was the weather that kept me indoors? "I . . . I don't get out much."

"Really? That's too bad."

"Why?" I asked. It was probably a dumb question, but I was curious about what he would say.

"There's good stuff out there."

"Like what?"

"Well . . ." He thought for a minute. "There's a nice park in the center of town. I spend a lot of time there."

"What do you do there?"

"Sit. Look. Think."

"Think about what?"

"Stuff. What do *you* think about?"

"Oh, books I've read. Movies."

"So you go out to movie theaters?"

"No. I wait till the films are on DVD so I can watch them at home."

"Oh. Right."

I must have sounded like a real drip. "And I think about what's out there," I said quickly. "What I've never seen. Tell me more about the park."

"It's big, a couple of square miles, I think. It takes up a big chunk of Midtown."

"Midtown," I repeated.

"The center of the city, where the businesses are.

Skyscrapers. And hotels, restaurants, nightclubs, places like that. The park's the only real green space in the area. There are a lot of trees. A lake, and a boathouse, where you can rent a canoe."

"Have you ever done that?"

"No. Wouldn't mind, though. I like watching the canoes. My favorite bench is by the lake. There's a children's playground at one end, with a merry-go-round. I loved riding it when I was a little kid. My old man used to bring me there on Sunday afternoons."

I imagined my own father taking a younger me to the park. People pointing, staring, laughing . . . I would have scared away kids like Max.

"In the spring," Max said, "there are a lot of flowers lining the paths."

"What kind of flowers?" I asked.

"Tulips, I think."

I caught my breath. "I love tulips. Especially yellow ones."

"Yeah? I'll have to remember that."

Was he suggesting that he might bring me a bouquet some time? That shivery thrill was fluttering through me again, sixty miles a minute.

"The park's really nice at night, too."

"It's not dangerous?"

"Nah, there are lights, and people take walks through it. It's kind of romantic. There's a big fountain, too, with a statue of an angel. People throw coins in the water for good luck. And there's a stand where you can get the best hot dogs in town."

"I've never had a hot dog," I told him.

"You're kidding! Huh. You ever have a beer?"

"Of course I've had a beer."

"A special Cloverdilly draft?"

"No, I don't think so."

"Then you've never had a real beer. And you can only get a Cloverdilly special draft at the Cloverdilly Pub, over on Orchard Street."

"Is that a nice place?"

"It's not fancy, if that's what you're thinking. Just an old-fashioned pub, packed with regulars. Good vibes."

There was a moment of silence. I tried to think of another subject. "Do you have any brothers or sisters?"

He hesitated, almost as if he wasn't sure. Then he said, "No. You?"

"No. That's something we have in common. It's not easy being an only child, is it? Lots of expectations."

He was looking uncomfortable. "Yeah, right."

My heart sank. I could tell that he wanted to leave. But just as I was about to tell him his time was up and give him an excuse to get out of here, he asked, "Do you play chess?" He was looking at the ornate, carved ivory set that was on the coffee table.

"Yes."

He examined the board. "It's all set up and ready. Want to play?"

"All right . . . but I'll play from here. You'll have to move the pieces for me."

"I think I can handle that. What's your opening move?"

"Um, pawn to king's four."

I watched as he moved the white pawn in front of my king forward two squares. Then he moved his black pawn opposite forward one square.

"Pawn to bishop's one," I said.

He obeyed, and thought for a minute before moving the pawn in front of one of his bishops forward two spaces. He was good, I thought. I was better. But in the end, when I took his king, he didn't mind.

"Okay, I owe you a Cloverdilly special draft," he declared. "Want to go out and get one?"

The question startled me. Was he joking? "Now?"

"Why not?"

"Um . . . no, thanks. Not now. Another time, okay?"

"When?" he asked.

"I'm not sure," I said carefully.

He looked at his watch and stood up. "I better get going."

I spoke quickly, before I could reconsider the question I was about to ask. "Will you come back? I mean, do you want to come back?"

He looked directly into the mirror, and again it felt like he was looking directly into my eyes.

"Yes. I do."

# Chapter Fifteen

Lemon was not happy.

"What the hell were you doing in there? You've been gone two hours!"

"I was worried," Edward chimed in. "We thought she ate you!"

Lemon shook his head. "You thought that, Vanderman, not me. What happened, Max?"

"We just got to talking, and . . ."

Edward somehow managed to appear horrified and lascivious at the same time. "*And* . . . ?"

Max shot him a dangerous look. "We talked."

Edward rolled his eyes. "Time flies when you're having a good time, huh?"

"And we played a game of chess," Max added.

"I don't care if you played hide the salami," Lemon growled. "All I want to know is, did you get the picture?"

"The picture?" Max echoed.

"The photo, Max! With the camera! Did you take a picture of Penelope?"

"Actually . . . no."

Lemon slammed his fist against the steering wheel and howled in pain. When he'd recovered, he fixed his one good eye on Max in aggravation. "Why not?"

"I know why not," Edward said suddenly. "He's double-crossing us!"

"How is he doing that?" Lemon asked.

Edward was getting visibly excited. "He wants more money! Right, Campion? You've already lost the five thousand bucks we gave you and now you think you can get more out of us!"

Max glared at him balefully. "I don't want any more of your money."

Edward widened his eyes in horror. "Wait, I get it now. You're going to propose to her! You're going to ask that pig-girl to marry you so you can get her dowry!" He shook his head in disbelief. "That's disgusting, what some people will do for money."

Lemon's brow furrowed. "Is that true, Max? Do you want to marry Penelope?"

"Don't ask stupid questions," Max muttered, but Lemon couldn't help noticing how he looked away as he spoke.

"This is ridiculous," Edward fumed. "I don't care what his motives are." He turned to Max. "If you're not going to get the photo, give us back the money and we'll find someone else to do it. I've got a reputation to salvage."

Lemon watched Max's face. The younger guy opened his mouth, then closed it. His eyes seemed focused on a spot way beyond anyone in the van. Obviously, something was going on in his head, and then Lemon recognized the expression. He'd been there before, when he was facing a particularly unpleasant assignment. Campion was battling some inner demons.

Lemon felt a sudden urge to ease his way.

"Look, Max, if you can't do it—"

Max blinked, then turned to Lemon. "No, I'll get it," he said with a grim determination. "Tomorrow."

# Chapter Sixteen

Max slid his remaining bishop diagonally across the board. "Check."

"Are you sure you want to do that?" I asked.

"I *think* so," he said. "Why?"

"My bishop takes your queen. Checkmate."

Max groaned. "That's three beers I owe you. If I can ever get you out of this place and over to the Cloverdilly so I can buy them for you."

I laughed. "You don't have to pay me off in beers, you know."

"How, then?"

"How about playing something on the piano for me?"

He was silent.

"Come on," I urged him. "You said you played."

"Used to," he corrected her.

"Oh, I'll bet it's like riding a bike," I said. "Even if it's been ages since you got on one, you pick it right back up."

"Have you ever been on a bike?" he asked.

"No," I admitted. "But I read that somewhere."

He gave me a crooked smile. "You can't believe everything you read."

There was another moment of silence.

"Why did you stop playing?" I asked him.

"Long story," he replied.

Something told me to change the subject. Actually, he'd been acting a little strange that day. Nice, as usual, and funny, but different. It was almost like he was nervous.

Or maybe that was just me, because I was feeling nervous, too. This was Max's third visit. How much longer could this relationship go on like this? And given the circumstances—did I even have the right to call it a relationship? All I knew for sure was that I'd never had these feelings before.

Suddenly, Max stood up. He turned, walked over to the piano, and sat down on the bench, his back to me. I watched as he flexed his hands and flinched when a knuckle cracked. He lifted the lid, and his hands hovered over the keys.

I waited in anticipation. A little jazz, maybe? Or something classical, maybe even romantic. Tchaikovsky, Rachmaninoff . . .

His fingers crashed down onto the keys, and he began pounding out "Chopsticks."

I laughed in delight. "Brilliant," I cried out.

I couldn't see his face, but he gave a real performance, with elaborate hand flourishes and head-tossing.

"Bravo!" I yelled when he finished. "Encore, encore!"

"I don't think I can top that," he said. "No, wait. I've got it." Dramatically, he raised his hands again.

What came out this time was another familiar melody, an introduction I recognized immediately. I was filled with a memory—sitting on the bench next to my father. He'd play the chords while I picked out the tune.

But Max was alone at the piano, so there could be no tune. He finished the introduction, and then started playing it again.

It was wrong like that, it was incomplete. Something was missing.

The chords became like musical magnets, tugging at me, drawing me against my will. Or maybe it *was* my will that propelled me, that pulled me off the loveseat and pushed me through the door. And then I was coming up behind him, closer, closer, and I could reach the keys.

Was he aware of me there, practically alongside him? He started the introduction again, and at the right moment I began to pick out the tune. I didn't sing along, but the words were running through my head as I hit each note.

*Heart and soul, I fell in love with you . . .*

I was looking at the keys, but he was looking at me, I

could feel it. With my heart pounding, I prepared myself for one of the old familiar expressions, and, slowly, I turned toward him.

I couldn't read his face at all. I didn't see shock, or horror, or fear . . . it was something else, an expression I couldn't identify. We both stopped playing, and the silence in the room was so complete it was almost surreal.

But not for long. My mother burst into the room with Wanda right behind her. "You!" she shrieked at Max. "Get out of this house!"

"Mother!" I exclaimed. I'd never seen her look quite this frenzied.

"You don't know what's going on, Penelope!" She pointed a trembling finger at Max. "It's a setup! That—that scoundrel—he's working with Lemon!"

The name didn't kick in immediately. "Who?"

"That sleazy journalist, that disgusting little weasel who wouldn't leave us alone!" Her shaking finger shifted to indicate the front of the house. "I saw him! He's out there right now, waiting in a van. I'm right, aren't I, Mr. Campion? This is a setup!"

I looked at Max. He'd gone completely pale. "Is this true, Max?" I asked him. "Is it a setup?"

"Get out of my house!" Mother screamed.

Wanda broke in. "Wait a minute, everyone. Who cares if it's a setup or not? Look what's happening here! He's seen her, and he's not running away! So what if he's a jerk? He meets the criteria, he's a blue blood, he can lift the spell! He doesn't have to be sincere, he doesn't even have to be nice. He just has to marry her!"

At least she'd managed to silence my mother. I looked at Max.

I liked him. I really liked him. And he hadn't run away from me. If there was an actual chance that I could be with a guy I really liked, I had to take a risk and let my feelings show.

"She's right, Max."

His eyes hadn't left my face, and his expression hadn't changed.

"Will you do it, Max?" I asked. "You could marry me and break the spell. Maybe I'm not the girl of your dreams right now, but once the spell is lifted, I'll be normal. Will you marry me?"

Suddenly, even before he spoke, I could identify the strange and mysterious expression on his face, and I was surprised I hadn't recognized it earlier. It was an emotion I knew well—sadness.

"What if I marry you, Penelope, but the curse remains?"

So that was why he looked so panicky. He was afraid he'd be stuck with the pig-girl forever.

"Then I'll kill myself," I said. "Really, I promise, that's what I'll do. You'll be free."

There was more than sadness in his eyes now. It was despair.

"I can't, Penelope. I'm sorry . . . but I can't."
Abruptly, he stood up and walked out of the room.

"Jake!" my mother shrieked. "Jake?" She ran out of
the room and Wanda followed. Her voice floated back
to the music room. "Jake, where are you? You have to
get a gag order and go after him!"

My father came in.

"Are you all right, my dear?"

"Yes," I said.

"Really?"

"I'm fine, Dad."

Strangely enough, this was the truth. I *was* fine. Fine
in a way that was very new for me. Because something
inside me had changed. "Excuse me, Dad. I think I'll
go lie down for a while."

He nodded understandingly. "I'll tell your mother
not to disturb you."

On the way to my bedroom, I stopped at a storage
closet. Inside, I found a small suitcase, and I took it to
my room. I placed the suitcase on my bed, opened it,
and went to my bureau, where I gathered some underwear, jeans, a couple of sweaters. From my bathroom
I collected a toothbrush and toothpaste.

Even though I never went outside, I owned a winter
coat, a very beautiful expensive one, that I bought in
preparation for my release from the witch's spell. It had
been sitting in my closet for seven years, and it was
probably out of style, but it would do.

There was a long scarf that matched the coat, too. Carefully, I wrapped it around my face, just high enough to cover my nose.

Next came the hardest part. I wasn't a criminal by nature, but drastic action called for drastic measures. I went to my parents' bedroom.

My mother's handbag was in its usual place on the night table. I fumbled around until I found her wallet. Then I took out a credit card. Putting it into my pocket, I went down the stairs and into the kitchen.

I was afraid my mother would be out front, taking out the journalist's other eye. So I slipped out the back.

# Chapter Seventeen

It wasn't difficult for Lemon and Edward to find Max. He was back in his old place, at a table in the back room of the Cloverdilly, with his usual gambling mates—the heavyset guy, the blue-haired lady, and the old man. When he saw Lemon and Edward walk in, he put his cards facedown on the table and got up.

"Look, I know what you're thinking," he said to them. "But I'm going to pay back the five grand as soon as I can win it."

"Yeah, sure you are," Edward muttered. "I won't hold my breath."

"Take it easy, Vanderman," Lemon muttered.

"He didn't even have the guts to come back to the van!" Edward protested.

"I wasn't in the mood," Max said.

Lemon shook his head wearily. "What's your problem? Didn't the camera work?"

"I don't know. I never tried to use it." Reaching inside his jacket, he took out the camera and handed it over. Then he took off the coat and tie and gave it to Lemon. "And you'll get the money, too."

Personally, Lemon thought the guy really looked like hell, worse than ever. His eyes weren't just tired, they were empty. Hollow.

The old man from the gambling table called out to Max. "Kid, you in?"

Max pushed a lock of hair out of his eyes. He looked at the card table for what seemed to be a long time. Finally, he shook his head. "No."

Brushing past Edward, he went into the main room of the bar. As Lemon watched, he took an empty paper cup from behind the bar, went over to the piano, and placed the cup on top of it. Then he sat down on the stool.

The bartender saw him and came out from behind the bar. "Hold it right there," he ordered. "Don't touch those keys. Sorry, man, but you know you're not our piano player anymore. Remember? I fired you for a reason."

Max spoke in a flat voice. "Maybe I've reformed."

"I don't think so, pal," the bartender said. "You know you can't keep away from the table. That's why I had to let you go. You were a pretty decent piano man, but you were never at the piano when you were supposed to be."

Slowly, Max nodded. "Right. But the thing is, I need a job." He nodded in Lemon's direction. "I owe this guy some money."

The bartender seemed to be considering that. He went to a closet and pulled out a broom. He extended it in Max's direction.

Lemon bit his lower lip. The whole scene was way too pathetic. "Look, pal, forget it," he said suddenly. "Don't worry about the money."

"What?" Edward yelped.

Lemon ignored him and continued speaking to Max. "It was the paper's money, not mine. Believe me, they can afford to lose it."

But Max had already risen from the piano stool and taken the broom from the bartender. "Thanks. You got an apron I can wear?"

Lemon turned away. "Come on, Vanderman."

"Great," Vanderman pouted as they left the Cloverdilly. "He's going to sweep floors. You know how long it will take him to make five thousand dollars?"

"What are you worried about? It's not your money," Lemon said. "Lay off him. Just . . . just forget it."

"Forget it? Are you kidding? Everyone still thinks I had a nervous breakdown! My father's not speaking to me. My mother wants to put me in a sanitarium. People in my office are still snickering when I walk by. I'm not giving up. We're going to get a photo."

Lemon shook his head. "I won't be able to get any more money out of the paper."

"You won't need to," Vanderman said. "I'll put up the bribe."

"And how are you going to find someone to take it?"
Vanderman shook his head wearily. "You're a journalist, right? Haven't you ever heard of the power of
the press? What does a half-page ad cost, anyway?"

# Chapter Eighteen

❧ ❧

I'd read about the outside world in books, and I'd seen it on TV. But nothing, *nothing*, could have prepared me for the reality of it.

People! So many people, coming and going, getting on and off buses, coming out of buildings. People jostling one another and me, too. People in thick coats, bundled up against the cold, with scarves wrapped around their faces—just like me! They could have all had pig faces, from what I could see of them.

And the noise! Cars honking, sirens wailing. A cacophony of voices. It was frightening. It was bewildering. It was magnificent.

I had no idea where I was, but the streets were lined with tall buildings, so I decided this had to be the Midtown Max had talked about. On the other side of the street, the sidewalk looked a little less crowded, so I decided to cross over. There was a squeal of brakes as a car swerved around me, and someone grabbed my arm.

"Lady, are you crazy? The light's red!"

I clutched my scarf to keep it from falling. Red lights, green lights, yes, I'd heard about those. You crossed on green and waited on red—or was it the other way around?

By the time I made it to the other side, I realized that with all this excitement, I'd ignored another sensation that was beginning to make itself felt. I was hungry.

I went into a shop and picked up candy bars, potato chips, a couple of sodas. Figuring I'd covered all the major food groups, I paid with my mother's credit card and went back out onto the street. The question now was, where could I eat my goodies? I couldn't get them into my mouth without taking my scarf off, and that was out of the question. I needed to find a place to stay.

It wasn't hard. Turning a corner, I saw the word HOTEL on a couple of buildings. I chose the bigger one and approached it. Standing by the entrance, a man in a uniform bowed to me and opened the door. That was nice and friendly, I thought. And the inside looked nice, too— lots of sofas and chairs placed in little conversational groupings. People were sitting in some of them and talking to one another. It seemed like a friendly sort of place.

I stood there, wondering what I was supposed to do. Then, from behind a long desk, a woman spoke to me. "May I help you?"

"Okay," I said happily.

There was a silence, and then she asked, "*How* can I help you?"

"I'm not sure."

"I'm sorry, but I can't hear you."

The scarf was muffling my voice. I moved closer to the desk.

"Would you like a room?" the woman asked.

"Yes! Yes, that's it. I want a room to stay in."

"Do you have a reservation?"

"Um, I don't know. I don't think so. What's a reservation?"

She looked at me oddly, and I didn't know if she hadn't heard me or if she didn't understand me. But her eyes swept over my expensive coat, and that seemed to assure her. "We do have a room available. Three twelve."

"Three twelve," I repeated. "Okay, thank you." I turned to go toward the elevator.

"Miss!"

I turned back. "Yes?"

"May I check you in?" She crooked a finger, indicating that I should come closer. "Your name?"

"Penelope Wilhern."

"I'm sorry, I really can't hear you."

I reached into my pocket and pulled out my mother's credit card. The woman took it from me.

"Jessica Wilhern." She must have recognized the name, because she looked impressed. "Very good, miss. And will you be using this card to pay for your room?"

I nodded.

"Very good, miss," she said again. She did something

with the card and handed me a paper to sign. I signed my mother's name, then a man appeared by my side and picked up my suitcase. I tried to grab it back.

"Stop, thief!" I yelled. Even with the scarf covering my mouth, no one had any problem hearing these words. Half the people in the room turned and looked at me.

"He's the porter, Miss Wilhern," the woman behind the desk said. "Would you prefer to take your suitcase to the room yourself?"

I nodded, and the man relinquished it to me. And the woman gave me a key. "Three twelve," she reminded me. As I turned away, I heard her whisper to the porter, "You know how eccentric these aristocrats can be."

After that, everything was easy. I found the room, the key opened the door, and once I was inside, I could take off my scarf and breathe normally. By now, I was starving. I whipped off my coat, opened my bag of goodies, and ate. It wasn't until after I'd stuffed myself that I saw the menu by the bed. Room service. They would deliver real food right to your room here! I'd have to remember that for next time.

The room was fine—I could live here permanently, I thought. The bed was huge, and there was more than enough room in the dresser and closet for the few things in my suitcase. In the bathroom was a Jacuzzi tub, and there was even a telephone on the wall just by it. Not that I had anyone to call.

I went over to the window and drew back the curtains.

The sun was going down and lights were coming on all over the city. It was all so new and strange, I could have been on another planet. A very, very beautiful planet . . .

Minutes earlier, I'd been utterly and completely exhausted. Now, I was exhilarated. I had to get out there and go . . . where?

The answer came to me quickly. The park. Max's park. He'd said it was wonderful at night. Just thinking his name gave me a pang, but I fought it back. I couldn't let myself brood. There was too much to do, to see, so much lost time to make up for.

There was a map in the room, and I looked it over. Just like Max said, the park took up a big chunk of Midtown, and it didn't seem too far away. I bundled up again, adjusted my scarf, and left the room.

The streets weren't as crowded now. I passed restaurants filled with people eating, theaters where people were lined up to buy tickets. And shops—amazing shops! I pressed my nose against the windows and gaped at the gorgeous clothes, shoes, handbags. It dawned on me that I could use my mother's credit card to buy these things. Tomorrow would be an adventure in shopping.

I forced myself away from the windows and kept walking. A few minutes later, I reached Max's park. I knew it was everyone's park, not just Max's, but that was how I thought of it. I wandered around until I thought I'd found his favorite bench, overlooking the lake.

There were soft lights illuminating the grounds. No

tulips, of course—it was still winter. And most of the trees were bare. But it was beautiful anyway. Still, and silent, and beautiful. I was really and truly outside, in the world.

Occasionally people walked by, but none of them paid any attention to me. They didn't seem to be paying any attention to where they were, either. How could they not look at everything in awe? It was a wonderland here, it was magic. All this time I'd thought I was living in a fairy tale. I was wrong. This—this park, this world—was the fairy tale. And it was real.

A man and a woman walked by, not speaking, just holding hands. Tears began to sting my eyes. This was the worst part of being still—you couldn't stop the thoughts from filling your head. Why had I thought that Max would be any different from all the others? Because he didn't scream when he saw my face? He just had more self-control than most men, that was all.

I didn't need Max. I didn't need any man. With the scarf around my face, hiding my nose, I could go anywhere, do anything, just like ordinary people. Maybe the witch's spell would never be broken. So what? As long as I had my scarf, I'd be fine.

But after a while I was getting hungry again, and I began to think about that room service menu. I walked back the way I came, and thought about snuggling up in that huge bed, turning on the TV, eating whatever I wanted.

I turned a corner, and the hotel loomed before me.

Home, I thought happily as I bounced up the steps and nodded at the man in uniform who was opening the door.

"Good evening, Miss Wilhern," he said.

He knew my name! The hotel really was beginning to feel like home. So much so that as I walked into the lobby, my imagination started playing tricks on me. I could almost hear my mother's voice.

"I demand to know what room she's in! It's my credit card that's paying for it!"

It wasn't my imagination. There they were, at the reception desk, talking to the woman who'd checked me in earlier. My mother and my father. The woman looked up and saw me. I didn't wait for my parents to turn around and do the same.

Running back out the door, I raced up the street. I took a right, then a left. People stared at me as I tore past them. They probably thought I was a bank robber, fleeing the scene of the holdup I'd just committed. They were practically right—I'd stolen a credit card, and it had come back to haunt me. Crime didn't pay.

I knew I couldn't go to another hotel. My mother would have reported the missing card, the hotel people would call the police, and someone would come after me. I had no money, no place to stay, I was hungry, and even bundled up, I was cold.

So I went back to the park, where it wasn't any warmer, but I thought I would find Max's bench again and I'd be able to think. When I got there, I saw that someone had left an open newspaper behind. I would have tossed it in the nearby trashcan, but something on the page caught my eye.

It was a drawing—very rough, like a sketch. A girl, no, more like a female monster, with fangs instead of teeth. And a nose like a pig's. Words over the picture screamed, "Have you seen this girl?"

I read on. A five-thousand-dollar reward was being offered to anyone who could provide the newspaper with an actual photo of the pig-girl. There was a phone number, and a name I recognized: Lemon.

I thought long and hard. Then I tore off the sheet, folded it carefully, and put it in my pocket.

Max had said something about a fountain where people threw in coins for good luck. I had to wander for a while, but eventually I found it. There weren't many coins—somebody probably cleaned the fountain out on a daily basis. But I was able to pick out some quarters, and I hoped that would be enough.

I remembered having passed a photo booth at the entrance to a subway, and I made my way back there. I went inside, closed the curtains, and took off my scarf. Then I put my quarters into the slot. Four times, a light flashed. I didn't have to wait long for the results.

I still had quarters left for a pay phone, and I dialed the number from the newspaper.

"Could I speak with Mr. Lemon, please? I have something he might be interested in."

# Chapter Nineteen

At nine in the morning, the Cloverdilly pub was pretty empty—just a couple of hard-core drinkers at the bar. Lemon assumed the back gambling room was busier.

But he didn't have to go there to find Max. He spotted the shaggy-haired guy at the other end of the room. He wore an apron, and he was sweeping the floor. Lemon was glad he'd been able to shake off Edward that morning. He could just imagine the sad SOB teasing Max about his new working uniform.

Actually, Lemon wasn't sure what he was doing here himself. There'd been a message on his desk that morning from Max, asking that Lemon meet him at the Cloverdilly. All he could think of was that maybe the guy had won some money in a game and wanted to pay back the five grand.

He studied the boy, who hadn't noticed him yet. He really seemed like a regular sort of guy. Something about the whole experience still didn't make sense. As he watched, the bartender approached Max.

"Hit the toilets next. They're a mess."

Max nodded, lifted the bucket of water, and trudged off into the restroom. Lemon felt a twinge of pity, which he forcibly brushed away. Why should he care if an impoverished aristocrat was reduced to scrubbing toilets? Max had been born with a silver spoon in his mouth, he'd blown the Campion fortune, he'd made his own bed. He wasn't worth feeling sorry for.

And yet, Lemon couldn't help feeling there was something, something *decent* about Max. Then he shook his head wryly at his own assessment. What did he, Lemon, know about decency? He'd spent his entire adult working life in this job, exploiting the unfortunate, exaggerating rumors, manipulating scandals. Integrity was not exactly his middle name.

He went over to the bar, ordered a coffee, and opened a newspaper that was lying there. While Lemon's paper had broken the story in the early morning edition, the other city newspapers had all picked it up by now. Headlines had varied: SHE'S REAL, THE WALKING, TALKING PIG, THE PIG-GIRL EXISTS! But all the articles carried the photos Lemon had picked up the evening before.

He still couldn't believe how it had happened. When he got the call at his paper, he thought it was a prank, and he'd been about to hang up on the muffled voice— and then he thought he heard something plaintive in the tone, and he continued to listen.

"This is Penelope Wilhern. I have some photos for you. Photos of me."

He was stunned. "Why do you want to give me photos of yourself?"

"I'm not *giving* them to you, I'm selling them. I want the five thousand dollars."

He was surprised when she explained why she needed the money, but the more he thought about it, the more sense it made. It was as if for the first time ever, he was realizing that she wasn't just some bizarre object of interest hidden away from view. And when he arrived at the designated meeting place, at midnight in the park, Penelope became even more real.

Not that he really saw her. She had told him to meet under a certain bridge, but she wasn't actually there.

"Lemon?" a voice called.

"Yes," he replied. He looked up and saw that she was standing on the bridge. At least, he assumed it was her. The figure on the bridge in the dark was heavily bundled and covered up.

She was holding what looked like a pail. Slowly, she lowered it down with a rope. Inside, there was a strip of photos. He took it out, put an envelope containing five thousand dollars in it, and gave it a jiggle. The pail was hoisted back up.

Lemon looked at the cheap grainy photo machine snapshots for a long time. They were not exactly what he expected to see.

He was looking at a person. Not a monster, not a freak, not a grotesque creature-from-the-black-lagoon. He saw a girl, a young woman, with pretty brown curly hair, big brown eyes, a wistful smile. The famous snout was there, of course, but he wasn't overcome with horror at the sight of it, just a little depressed. He looked up from the photos, but Penelope had disappeared.

Now, sitting at the bar, looking at the grainy newspaper version of the photos, he tried to cheer himself by thinking of the girl's mother, that evil harridan who took out his eye. She had to be suffering now, with the face of her pig-daughter in every newspaper, exposed to the world. Funny, though, how the image didn't give him the kind of gratification he'd thought it would.

"Are you happy now?"

Lemon looked up to see Max standing by his bar stool. The younger man's face was grim.

"How's it going, Campion?"

Max didn't answer the question. "You couldn't leave her alone, could you? You had to have your revenge. Nothing was going to keep you from your damned exposé. You had to hound her, you had to have that picture, you had to embarrass her publicly. I know you hate the mother, I know she screwed up your life, but why did you have to take it out on Penelope? What did she ever do to you?"

Lemon tried to break into the tirade. "Whoa, hold on there—"

But Max wasn't finished. "You make me sick, you and Vanderman. Okay, Vanderman's an ass, but you— you're even worse. You don't even know the girl. Why did you want to hurt her?"

Lemon couldn't let this go by. "Why did *I* want to hurt her? What about you? You're no better than me *or* Vanderman. I think you'd better step down from your moral high ground, my boy."

Max stared at him. "What's that supposed to mean, Lemon?"

"You could have helped her, you could have changed her life. You could have married her and lifted that stupid curse. You had the means to make Penelope Wilhern happy, but you didn't. And I know why."

There was uncertainty in Max's eyes. "You do?"

"You're no better than Vanderman. You were grossed out by her face."

Max looked away, and Lemon pressed his point. "Actually, come to think of it, you're *worse* than Vanderman. Because I think you like the girl. Maybe you even love her. But you can't deal with the snout. You're just as shallow as all those other guys who ran away."

Was he getting through to Max? There was no expression at all on the boy's face, and he'd made no attempt to defend himself.

"And I'm going to tell you something else, too." Lemon tapped the photo. "It was Penelope herself who gave me these pictures."

*That* got a reaction. Max's mouth fell open. "What?"

"She called me last night and offered them to me."

Max narrowed his eyes. "I don't get it. Why would she do that?"

"She wanted the money. No, it was more than that. She *needed* the money."

"That's crazy. You're not making any sense. She's a Wilhern—they're loaded."

Lemon played his trump card. "It seems our Penelope has made a change in her lifestyle. She left home."

Max seemed to have gone speechless. It took several seconds before he could even manage a weak "You're kidding."

"She's out there right now, Campion. I don't know where she's staying or what she's doing, but she broke out. Penelope Wilhern is on her own. She's declared her independence."

There was another moment of silence. "Huh. How 'bout that." Then a slow smile spread across Max's face. "Good for her."

The bartender came down to their end of the bar. "You finished for the day?"

"Yep," Max replied.

The bartender opened the cash register and counted out some bills. "There you are. Thanks."

Just then a man appeared in the doorway leading to the back room. Lemon recognized him as one of Max's gambling partners.

"Hey, we got an empty chair back here."

Max shook his head. "No thanks, man." He extended the money to Lemon. "An installment on my debt."

Lemon didn't want to take it. But he had a feeling he'd be insulting Max if he didn't. "Thank you." He stuffed the bills in his pocket as Max put the broom back in the closet, took off the apron, and ambled out of the bar.

# Chapter Twenty

❦～❦

Control. It was a completely new sensation, something I'd never felt before. I—not my mother, my father, Wanda, or Jake—was in control of my life. I, Penelope Wilhern, was making the decisions, calling the shots. It was scary, it was bewildering . . . it was wonderful.

Of course, the room I woke up in that morning couldn't compare to the room at the grand hotel or to my room back at the Wilhern mansion. After getting the money from Lemon, I walked through the Midtown streets and eventually found a shabby-looking building with a ROOMS FOR RENT sign in a window. The bed was lumpy, the wallpaper was faded and peeling, there was no TV or phone or fabulous view from the tiny window, but I'd been able to put a month's deposit down in cash and still had plenty left.

And they'd never come looking for me here. Some people might look at this place and say, she's come down in the world. Not me, though. I'd say, she's taken her first step up, out, and into the world.

I dressed quickly, wrapped the scarf around my face, and left the room. Outside, I merged with the crowds on the streets and set off to explore. Window shopping was great fun. Without my mother's credit card, I knew I'd have to watch my budget, but I made mental notes of certain shops that displayed some gorgeous clothes.

On the other hand, when I passed a group of women in chadors and face veils, I wondered if that might be something that would work for me. I'd probably have to become a Muslim, and wearing black all the time couldn't be too exciting, but it would resolve the issues regarding the exposure of my face. It was another option, and that was what I found so thrilling—all the possibilities I was encountering.

I was intrigued by the beauty salons I passed, too, and considered the prospect of cutting my long hair. I could also have a manicure—the possibilities were endless!

What else could I do with my money? I could buy a TV for my little room, but I decided against that. My days of watching life on a screen were over. I was living life now.

I did invest in a little combination radio/alarm clock, though. I was hoping my bright new future would bring things I would need to get up on time for; plus I wanted music, a soundtrack for my new life.

When I felt myself getting hungry, I discovered fast-food restaurants. The concept was incredible—you could walk into one of these places, get hamburgers, chicken, French fries, and then take it all away to eat anywhere you wanted! I didn't particularly feel like going back to my room, so I went to the park, sat on a bench, and figured out a way to eat. I extended the scarf outward from my mouth with one hand and used the other to poke French fries under it. A couple of passersby glanced at me oddly, but no one could see anything really disgusting.

After lunch, I went back to exploring and wandering. At one point, I realized I was on Orchard Street. The name rang a bell, and I didn't have to think long and hard to remember where I'd heard of it. Max's favorite pub, the Cloverdilly, was on Orchard. And after walking along for a few minutes, I saw the sign just ahead.

I hesitated. I wanted to check it out, but what if Max was in there? I didn't think I was ready for an encounter, not yet. Maybe not ever. I edged over to the door and peered inside. He wasn't at the bar. Was I relieved or disappointed? I really couldn't say.

But I went on in and sat down on a bar stool. The guy behind the bar gave me a friendly smile. "Hi, what can I get you?"

I remembered what Max had recommended. "A Cloverdilly special draft, please."

"Coming right up."

I watched him put a huge mug under a pump and pull down a lever. Golden foamy beer filled the mug. Then he set it down and pushed it. It slid down the bar, picking up speed on the slick surface until it passed me, fell off the edge, and crashed on the floor.

"You were supposed to catch it," the bartender said.

I felt like a moron. "Sorry. I guess it's been a while since I had a beer on tap."

He grinned. "No problem. It all comes back to you."

"Like riding a bike?"

"Exactly." He poured me another beer and sent it down the bar. This time I grabbed it. But now I was faced with another obstacle. Drinking with my mouth covered presented a graver problem than eating. I made a futile attempt to get the lip of the mug under the scarf.

The bartender watched me curiously. "Would this help?" he asked. He handed over a straw.

"Thank you," I said gratefully. I stuck the straw into the beer, poked the other end under my scarf, and sucked up the best beer I've ever tasted. As I drank, my eyes went to an open newspaper lying on the bar, and I almost choked. There I was, in all my radiant glory. But no one at the bar was making the connection between me and the freak in the photo—so what did I care? I took another long, delicious sip.

The door to the Cloverdilly swung open, and a pretty

blond-haired woman carrying a helmet in one hand and a box in the other sauntered in.

"Yo, Annie baby." The bartender leaned over the bar to kiss her cheek. "Ya got something for me?"

"My last delivery of the day," she said, dropping the package on the bar. "And I would kill for a beer."

"But you don't have to," the bartender said. He opened a bottle and handed it to her. "On the house."

"Love ya, man." She took the stool next to me, glanced in my direction, and lifted her bottle. "Cheers."

"Cheers," I murmured.

She took a long, thirsty gulp, put the bottle down, and looked at me again. "Nose job?"

"What?"

"I'm guessing you just had a nose job. What's the medical word for it—rhinoplasty? I always thought that was funny. I mean, it's like all the patients had noses like a rhino before getting it fixed."

Close, I thought. But I just nodded.

Annie continued. "A girlfriend of mine, she had a nose job, and she wore a scarf like that for three weeks. At first, she went out with her bandages showing, but everyone kept asking her if she'd been in an accident and being sorry for her. She felt guilty getting so much sympathy from people when it was all just for vanity's sake."

I nodded again.

"Not that there's anything wrong with vanity," Annie went on. She tugged at a lock of hair. "When I see the tiniest trace of roots coming in, I'm at Ronaldo's."

I raised my eyebrows.

"You don't know Ronaldo? Best hairdresser in town, he costs a fortune but he's worth it." She cocked her head and studied my hair. "You've got a blunt cut, so I guess you don't have to go to that kind of salon. Just about anyone can cut straight across, right? Must save you money, having a style like that."

I gathered up the nerve to speak. "It does. My mother's always cut it for me." Geez, I sounded like a baby. I didn't want to put this girl off me.

"Does it hurt?"

"When my mother cuts my hair?"

She laughed. "No, I'm talking about the nose job again. Sorry about that, I'm all over the place."

"That's okay," I said quickly. "No, it doesn't hurt."

"Really?" She looked incredulous. "Not at all?"

Was a nose job supposed to hurt? "I mean, not very much."

"Because I'm thinking about getting one myself."

"Why? Your nose is fine."

She glanced at the open newspaper. "Well, I'm no Penelope, that's for sure. Mine's just a little crooked. But I'm really talking about my ears."

"You want to have a nose job on your ears?" As soon as the words left my mouth, I realized how stupid they sounded, and I wanted to kick myself. But Annie laughed in delight, as if I'd just said something incredibly funny.

"I always thought my ears stuck out," Annie told me. "It's kind of silly, though, cosmetic surgery. Who's to say what makes beautiful ears or a beautiful nose? I mean, who made the rules?"

"Not me," I said.

"Me neither." She raised her bottle and clinked it against my mug. "Hey, Sam!" she called to the bartender. "How about a couple more for me and my new friend here?"

Maybe I'd been drinking the beer too fast, but a little thrill went through me. Nobody had ever called me a friend before. Well, except Edward Vanderman. But I couldn't take anything he'd ever said to me seriously.

We clinked our new beers together, and then Annie said, "You're not from around here, are you, Scarfie?"

"No," I said. "I'm from . . . France. *Bonjour.*"

"I want to travel," Annie said. "You know what my fantasy is? I want to get on my Vespa and go all over the country."

"Your Vespa?" I asked.

"You don't know what a Vespa is?"

Embarrassed, I shook my head again. But Annie seemed to accept my ignorance as just another aspect of being a foreigner. She finished her beer and gazed mournfully at the empty bottle. "I could drink another, but then I shouldn't drive. And it's so gorgeous out."

"The sun's shining," I noted.

"Yeah. It's still pretty cold, but spring's on its way. I saw a few tulips in the park this morning."

"Really? Tulips are my favorite flowers."

"I've got an idea," Annie said. She slapped her bottle down on the bar. "I'm through with my deliveries for the day. Want to cruise around town with me? We could check out those tulips. And it would be a lot healthier than sitting here boozing all day. You up for it?"

I wished Annie could see my huge smile. "Yes."

Outside, I found out what a Vespa was. Having never been on any kind of a motorcycle, I was a little apprehensive, but I tried to act cool as Annie helped me put on her spare helmet. I got on the back, and we took off.

What a feeling! Another brand-new experience. I felt like I was flying. It was a thrilling and exhilarating sensation. I wanted it to go on forever, and when Annie began to slow down, I cried out, "Don't stop!"

Annie threw back her head and laughed. "I have to, it's a red light! Don't worry, we'll move again." As we took off, she began giving me a tour of the city.

"See that church? It's the oldest building in town. That's City Hall on the right. I've been there quite a few times."

"You know the mayor?" I asked.

"No, but I'm very chummy with the folks in the Department of Motor Vehicles." She laughed, and I didn't understand the joke, but I laughed, too. There was just something about Annie that made me feel like laughing.

"That's my favorite sculpture," she said, pointing out a strange lumpy mound of marble.

"It's weird," I said.

"Yeah, but weird can be beautiful, y'know?"

I wasn't sure about that. "What's that big building over there?" I asked.

"The Museum of Natural History. Cool dinosaur skeletons. Kids love it. You have kids?"

"No," I said.

"Me neither. I want to have them someday. But I'd like to find a husband first. I'm old-fashioned that way. It's not easy meeting the right kind of guys, though, you know what I mean?"

"Oh, I do," I said fervently.

We were heading out of Midtown into the residential area now, and I was alarmed when Annie turned down my old street. I had on the scarf and the helmet, but even so, I turned my head just in case my mother happened to be looking out the window.

"This is the ritziest part of town," Annie explained. "Nice shacks, huh?"

"Mm."

She stopped, right in front of the Wilhern mansion. "I can't imagine what it's like to live in a house like that. I guess you'd feel like a princess. These people must be incredibly rich."

"Yeah."

"But do you think they're happy?" Annie asked.

"I don't know," I said. All I knew was, right at that very minute I was happier than I'd ever been living in that house.

# Chapter Twenty-one

"Gooooood morning, all you lovely people!" bellowed the deejay. "Get those butts out of bed and take to the streets, because there's something special waiting out there for you today, and it's going to be a big surprise! Overnight, out of the blue, without any warning, spring has sprung!"

I rolled over and turned to look at the clock radio. Then I leaped out of bed. I was supposed to meet Annie in ten minutes. We were going to hit the botanical gardens today, and I didn't want to be late. It was amazing—here I was, a lover of plants, and I hadn't even known there was such a place in the city. Annie was opening my eyes to a great big beautiful world I never knew existed.

I hurried to shower and dress. Maybe I'd never had a real friend before, but one thing I knew—you didn't keep a friend waiting. Wrapping my scarf carefully and securely around my face, I was ready to go.

I was walking quickly and thinking about the day

ahead, so maybe that was why it took a few minutes before I sensed that something was different today. As I hurried along, I noticed that several passersby glanced at me curiously. I touched my scarf to make sure it hadn't shifted and I was exposing myself. But it wasn't my snout they were noticing—it was the scarf itself. Because there was no reason to wear a scarf today. Or a big, heavy coat. There was no chill in the air, no biting wind.

The words of the radio deejay came back to me—something about "spring has sprung." As beads of sweat formed on my brow, I finally understood what he meant. There'd been a change in the weather. Even if I hadn't already started to feel uncomfortably warm, I could see evidence of the climate change in the people I passed on the streets. The fur coats, the woolen hats, and the puffy ski jackets had disappeared. I saw raincoats and sweaters, and some people didn't have on any outerwear at all. And no one was wearing a scarf.

I wasn't stupid. And even though I'd been an indoor person, I knew about the seasons. I must have known that eventually a woolen scarf wrapped around my face wouldn't work as a year-round accessory. But I'd blocked it out, or refused to think about it, or something. And now I was faced with the fact.

Then, just as I was struggling with the magnitude of this brand-new dilemma, another problem appeared. Actually, the problem was audible before it was visible.

The voice pierced my entire being and stuck me right in the gut.

"Franklin, Franklin! Look! It's her! It's Penelope! Penelope!"

Needless to say, I didn't have to turn around to identify the source of the shrieking voice. I responded automatically—I just took off running.

Amazing how the adrenaline kicked in. I never knew I could even run this fast. My legs felt motorized. They couldn't catch up with me, but even so I knew they were trailing me. My mother's cries became fainter, but I could still hear them, which wasn't a good sign.

My heart was pounding furiously, and the sweat was pouring off me. The scarf around my face was wet and clammy, sticking to me like a damp sponge. Waves of nausea passed through me.

I made out the sign of the Cloverdilly, just a block ahead. By now I was feeling truly sick. I was shaking as I ran and my legs had turned to jelly. Somehow, someway, dizzy and weak and stumbling, I staggered into the pub.

"There you are, Scarfie!" Annie called out. And then, in a different tone: "What's the matter?"

I'd stopped running but the room was spinning faster and faster, and I felt myself become weightless. Dim cries surrounded me.

"She's passing out!"

"Call an ambulance!"

"Dial nine-one-one!"

The next minute, I wasn't sure if I'd fallen or if the floor had risen to meet me. Was the room going dark or had I closed my eyes?

"Stand back, give her air!" I recognized Annie's voice. Then I felt a hand on my face, and I knew it was unwrapping my scarf.

I wanted to cry "No, no," but I couldn't speak. But then I heard that familiar shriek, and it was screaming what I was thinking.

"No, no! Stop, don't do it!"

I was fading away. My last sensation was a blast of air on my bare face. And the last voice I heard was Annie's surprised exclamation.

"Penelope!"

# Chapter Twenty-two

I opened my eyes.

"Where am I?"

A pleasant but unfamiliar voice responded, "You're in the hospital, Miss Wilhern. Now, don't worry, there doesn't seem to be anything seriously wrong with you. But you fainted, and the doctors just want to check you out before they discharge you."

I was still lying flat on my back and staring up at the white ceiling. It was all coming back to me, too clearly. The heat, running from my parents, the Cloverdilly, feeling sick. The scarf . . . there was no need for me to touch my face to know that it was gone. The ramifications, implications, and repercussions of what had happened rushed over me. It was too much. I closed my eyes.

"Miss Wilhern? Are you feeling all right? I'll get the doctor."

I forced my eyes open again. "No, I'm okay." Then I struggled to an upright position and turned to the wall so the poor nurse wouldn't have to see my face. Unfortunately, the wall turned out to be a window. Reporters' mouths were moving, bright lights flashed as waiting photographers took pictures, and one reporter was able to yell loud enough for me to hear him through the glass.

"Penelope! Is it true you were kept prisoner in a basement for twenty-five years?"

"Penelope, do you have a curly tail?"

Briskly, the nurse went to the window and drew the curtains. "I'm sorry about that. It's crazy around here. The hospital's been surrounded by reporters and photographers since you arrived."

I sank back onto the pillow. So this was it. It was all over for me. The worst had gotten even worse. They not only knew I existed—now they knew where I was.

I was barely aware of the nurse taking my temperature and checking my pulse and my blood pressure. My mind was a blank. I had no idea what could possibly happen next. I was so confused and bewildered that it was almost—*almost*—a relief when my mother came into the room, followed by my father.

At least the hospital environment had caused Jessica to lower her voice. "Oh my poor darling," she murmured, hurrying to my bedside. "My poor child."

What could I say? *It's not the end of the world?* I thought I was pretty safe in assuming I wouldn't be able to convince her of that.

"How do you feel, sweetheart?" my father asked anxiously.

"I feel all right," I said. "Can we leave? I want to get out of here."

My mother glanced fearfully at the window. Reporters were yelling, "Penelope, Penelope!"

"Well, you can't leave here right now, dear. I've asked the hospital administrators to escort us through a back service door."

I sighed. "Oh, Mother, why bother? It's too late for all that."

"Now, now, don't worry, Penelope, don't despair, everything's going to be fine," she assured me. "Daddy is going to buy us a deserted island somewhere in the middle of nowhere."

There was a knock on the door. "Franklin, lock it!" she screamed. But the door opened before my father could reach it, and a man in a white coat entered. "Get out of here!" she yelled.

The man glared at her. "I'm the doctor. *You're* the one who's not supposed to be in this room. Out!"

At least my mother realized this was one place where she couldn't be in charge. She and my father left.

"Well, Miss Wilhern," the doctor said. "Everything about you checks out fine. In fact, you're in excellent health. You're completely normal."

"Normal?" I asked skeptically, and I touched my snout. Just in case he hadn't noticed.

"Well, there is *that,* of course. It's a very interesting anomaly. But other than the fact that your carotid artery runs through it, your snout doesn't have any impact on your general physical health. You just became over-heated, and that was what caused you to faint. There's no reason for you to stay in the hospital."

"Thank you, Doctor."

"Shall I send your family back in?"

"No thank you, Doctor."

Having spent a few seconds in the presence of Jessica Wilhern, he smiled in complete understanding and left. I took off the hospital gown and put on the clothes I'd worn that morning, with one exception. No scarf. What was the point now?

There was another knock on the door. I wasn't surprised—I was sure my mother would find her way back here once the doctor had left the corridor. "Come in, Mom," I said in resignation.

Only it wasn't my mother. A man in a trench coat slipped in and pulled a notebook out of his pocket. "Penelope, just a few questions, *please.*"

I groaned—he was obviously a reporter. "Oh, can't you just leave me alone?" I began, and then I stopped. There was something very odd about the way he was looking at me. Not in shock, terror, horror, fear, disgust—not even in sympathy. He was interested. More than interested—he was fascinated by me.

"What do you want to know?" I asked cautiously.

"How does it feel?"

"I feel fine."

"No, I mean your . . . your snout . . . excuse me, I'm sorry, your nose . . . whatever you call it. How does it feel?"

"That feels fine, too."

"But, but . . . what's it like? What does it do? How do you smell?"

I took an experimental sniff of my wrist. "Like Chanel Number Five."

The reporter grinned and jotted that down.

"Excuse me," I said, moving past him and out the door. My parents came hurrying down the corridor toward me. My mother was carrying a big silk scarf she must have just bought in the hospital gift shop.

"This way, darling, we're going down to the delivery entrance." She started arranging the scarf around my face but I pushed her hand away.

"No, I think I'll go out the front door, like normal people. How's my hair?"

For the first time in my life, I had rendered Jessica Wilhern speechless. I took advantage of the fact.

"Mom, Dad, I have to tell you something. Something very important."

My father looked alarmed and Mother clutched her throat. "What, Penelope?"

"I don't want to live on an island."

While they absorbed that information, I walked right

past them and out the front door. Cameras clicked and a yell went up from the gang of reporters who rushed to converge at the bottom of the steps.

"Penelope, how did you manage to keep yourself a secret for twenty-five years?"

"Were you chained up in an attic or a basement?"

"What are you going to do now?"

By now, my parents had recovered from my announcement and were at my side. "Can't you leave her alone?" my mother pleaded.

"It's okay, Mom," I said. "I can handle this."

"Penelope, do you have anything to say to the world?"

I thought for a minute. "Hi." That was when I spotted Annie, on her Vespa, waiting in front of the building. She waved the spare helmet toward me.

I went down the steps. "Later, guys, okay?" The reporters actually parted like the Red Sea for me, giving me the space to get to the street and to Annie. Slipping on the helmet, I climbed on the back of the Vespa.

I'd thought it was all over for me. I was wrong. It was all beginning.

# Chapter Twenty-three

Annie had given me a scrapbook, and the first few pages were already filled with things she'd pasted into it. Unlike the old Wilhern family scrapbook, this one was all about me. There were photos, fan mail, a cute little caricature drawing from an artist. I'd been out of the hospital and back in my little rented room for almost a week, and the building manager had started dumping my mail at my door since the mailbox downstairs was too small.

Sitting on the bed, I spread out the clippings and other stuff I needed to put in the scrapbook. PENELOPE SAYS "HI," declared the headline that accompanied the photo of me leaving the hospital. There were follow-up articles from the same newspaper—PENELOPE DENIES RUMORS OF ABUSE ("I don't blame my parents—they did what they thought was best for me"), SALES OF CHANEL NUMBER FIVE SKYROCKET ("This is what Penelope smells like!"), NEW HYBRID SNOUT-SHAPED TULIP NAMED PENELOPE. On the gossip and entertainment page, there was a picture of me with my arms full of shopping bags (THIS LITTLE PIGGY GOES TO MARKET!).

When I finished pasting in the photos and clippings, I started opening the stack of mail. There were invitations—one was to a fund-raiser given by the Society for the Prevention of Cruelty to Animals, another was to a gay rights benefit ("Penelope came out of her closet, you can come out of yours"), and a request to use my name for a half-girl, half-pig Penelope doll.

There was a rap on my door followed by a call of "It's me!"

"Come on in, Annie," I called out.

She looked fabulous—hair piled on top of her head, gold glitter minidress, sky-high heels. We were going to a disco, another first for me. And not just any disco—we were actually going to try to get into the most exclusive club, where models and playboys hung out. "Ready?" she said.

"Just about." I hopped off the bed and checked my reflection in the mirror. My outfit was pretty hot, too, red and slinky and cut-down-to-there.

"Have you seen this?" Annie opened a magazine she was carrying. Under the heading "Celebrity Central," there I was, on the same page as royalty and movie stars.

"Thanks." I put it in my scrapbook pile, and we left the room. As usual, outside the building there were a couple of young preteen girls wanting autographs.

After I signed and they took off, Annie said, "You're

going to have to start disguising yourself, like movie stars with sunglasses. Maybe you could invent noseglasses."

I felt sort of embarrassed. "I don't know, Annie. Sometimes I feel like a fraud."

"What do you mean?"

"They're making all this fuss about me, and it's just because of my nose."

Annie gave a nonchalant shrug. "So what? Your nose is a part of who you are."

"But that's just it," I said. "It isn't a part of who I am. This isn't my face. It's the curse."

She'd heard the whole story by now, of course. She knew all about Great-great-great-grandfather Ralph and Clara and the witch, how I'd been hidden for twenty-five years, how I needed a man "of my own kind" to marry me for the curse to be broken.

"Sometimes I feel like I'm going to spend my whole life just waiting for someone to lift this curse."

Annie laughed. "Hey, don't knock it. Your nose is going to get us into the hottest club in town. And there should be a lot of cool guys in there."

"But how will I know if any of them are blue bloods?" I wondered worriedly.

"Girlfriend, why don't you just try to relax, have a good time, and not worry about finding a husband to-night?" Annie suggested.

"*If* we get in," I reminded her. "You're so pretty, you could get into any chic place, but me . . ."

"Are you kidding?" Annie laughed. "Penelope, you're a star! *I'll* get in tonight because I'm with *you*!"

Sure enough, the bouncer at the door of the club was lifting the velvet rope and beckoning us forward. The people who were waiting to get in cheered and applauded. Maybe Annie had a point. This wasn't me—but at least no one was running away from whoever I was.

Inside, the club was spectacular, huge, all purple and silver and flashing lights. The music was blasting, and all over the place were beautiful people, dancing and drinking and laughing. I recognized several faces from movies and TV, and I was sure I had a goofy expression on my face as I looked around in awe.

"I guess I should act more casual," I screamed into Annie's ear. "I know it's not supposed to be cool to stare at famous people."

"Why not?" Annie screamed back. "They're staring at *you*."

She was right. As my eyes adjusted to the crazy lighting in the club, I could see that a lot of people, even some of the celebrities, were staring right back at me. And with the same awestruck expression that I felt pretty sure was plastered on my face.

We made it over to the bar, where we ordered our drinks. The bartender refused to take our money. "It's an honor to have you here, Penelope," he said.

For someone who'd been living in solitude for twenty-five years, all this attention was difficult to handle. Annie understood this, and we moved around the dance floor to a table in a corner, where I could be less conspicuous. I did notice a couple of very hot guys looking in our direction, though. Annie saw them, too.

"Not bad, huh?"

I nodded. "I think they're checking you out."

"How do you know they're not checking *you* out?" Annie countered.

It was sweet of her to say that, but these guys didn't seem the types who were interested in a pig, not even a celebrity pig. One of them looked like a surfer dude, blond and tan and lanky. He wore a tank top that showed off sinewy arms. The other one had long dark hair, a diamond stud in one ear, and looked like a rock star. I thought I'd died and gone to cute-guy heaven.

"They're coming over," Annie declared happily. "I hope you're feeling flirty."

"I don't know what to say to them," I said nervously. "I don't have any flirting experience."

"Well, I know this sounds corny and like something a mother would say, but just be yourself."

I wanted to laugh. "Annie, my mother would never say that to me. How can I be myself when I'm not myself?"

"Sorry, that's a little too existential for me," Annie said. "Hello, boys. Have a seat or two."

They pulled over chairs and joined us at the table. "So, how's it going?" Surfer Dude asked.

"It's going fine," Annie replied. She gave me a look that said *speak*.

"Yes, it's fine with me, too."

The Rock Star spoke. "I'm Steve. This is Mike." He looked directly at me. "And you're Penelope."

Desperately, I tried to think of something more clever to say than *yes*. "Oink," I replied.

It was pretty feeble, and Annie rolled her eyes at me, but the guys laughed as if I'd been sparkling and witty. After a few minutes more of chatting, I realized why. They were both utterly boring, wit-free, and conversationally challenged. Annie took action.

"Hey, Penelope, look at those girls who just came in. They look so familiar. Is there a top-model convention in town?"

The boys leaped up from their chairs and took off. I searched the crowd in the direction Annie had been looking. "I don't see any top models."

"That's because they're not there. I was just trying to get rid of them."

"Why?" I asked.

"Didn't you think they were stupid?"

"Well, sure," I said. "But the dark-haired one, I think he kind of liked me."

Annie looked at me thoughtfully. "Did you like him?"

"Not particularly, but . . ." I remembered what Wanda had once said. "Beggars can't be choosers. And pigs can't be picky."

"You're not a beggar, Penelope. Or a pig."

"Easy for you to say," I replied. "You're beautiful."

Annie didn't try to deny it. "I'm pretty," she said. "You're unique."

"Because I have the face of a pig. Which has nothing to do with who I really am."

Annie groaned. "Okay, who *are* you, Penelope? And don't give me that story about your great-great-great-grandfather and the witch again. I'm asking who you really are, deep inside where it counts."

"How should I know? I *told* you, I won't know who I am until I'm married and I become myself."

Annie studied her beer. "I almost got married once."

"Really?"

She nodded. "I was engaged. Joe was a nice guy. Smart, decent looking. He had a good job, he wasn't an alcoholic or a druggie or anything like that. And I wanted to be married. You know why?"

"Because you had a pig face?" I joked.

She didn't laugh. "Yeah, in a way. I thought I was nobody, and I had to get married to be someone. You know, Mrs. So-and-So. Some guy had to want me."

"What happened?" I asked her.

"I got smart, just in time," she said. "I looked at friends who got married, and I realized that they were the same people they'd been when they were single. And I realized something else, too." She smiled. "I was already someone, I'd been someone all along. And I wasn't in love with Joe, which meant I'd be using him if I married him just to change myself. Which wouldn't happen anyway because I didn't need to change. Does that make sense?"

"It's a little transcendental," I told her. "I'll have to think about it."

"The thing is," she said, "you have to stop thinking about what you *will* be, and just be."

"Now you're going way over my head," I said. "Why don't we have a couple more beers and talk about something easy?"

# Chapter Twenty-four

This wasn't the kind of assignment Lemon particu-larly liked. Finance wasn't his thing, and covering the announcement of a merger didn't sound like much fun. But it was considered a prestigious assignment at his newspaper, and lately the editor had been rewarding him with so-called plums like this. Discovering Penelope had finally given him a notable name in journalism circles.

It was incredible. Within a week, the girl had gone from being a well-kept secret to a celebrity. Penelope was everywhere. Paparazzi followed her, and any photogra-pher lucky enough to get a candid shot was pulling in a fortune. Her views on everything from fashion to politics were sought and reported. Just that morning, Lemon had seen a health-and-fitness magazine with a picture of Penelope on the cover and a banner reading SHE'S NO PIG! HOW PENELOPE KEEPS HER FABULOUS FIGURE.

He joined colleagues from other newspapers who had already gathered for the press conference at Vanderman Industries. They greeted him with a warmth and respect he'd never known before—something else he could thank Penelope for. If he ever saw her again. By now, she was being courted by the big-time papers, the high-circulation mags, and rumor had it that *60 Minutes, Dateline,* and *20/20* were in a three-way struggle over who would get the first televised interview. Penelope was now out of his league. He just hoped she was happy.

"Good afternoon, ladies and gentlemen of the press, I am Edward Vanderman Senior."

Lemon grinned. It wasn't that common for a man to use "senior" in his name, unless he was trying very hard to distinguish himself from his "junior." Sure enough, the younger Vanderman was sitting on the podium with some other men in suits.

The father continued. "I have called you here today to announce the merger of Vanderman Industries with Clifton Enterprises, which will become known as Vanderman Enterprises. We are awaiting the approval of federal agencies, but of course, as a publicly traded company, our main concern is the reaction of our shareholders."

Blah, blah, blah, boring, boring, boring, Lemon thought. He actually thought longingly of the days when he was working on Elvis sightings, or tracking down an image of the Virgin Mary on a microwave oven.

"According to Wall Street analysts, the impact of this merger on the stock exchange . . ."

Lemon tuned out. He was more interested in looking at Vanderman Junior and contemplating what might be going on in his head. They hadn't had any contact since the ad for Penelope's pictures was placed. He wondered how Edward felt, now that the world finally knew he'd really seen a girl with the face of a pig and hadn't had a nervous breakdown. Had he finally won his father's approval and respect?

And how did he feel when he saw Penelope's face everywhere? Lemon remembered what Edward had been like that first day they met in the police station. The poor fellow had been shaking; he'd been in a state of shock. What was it like for him now? Did he start shaking every time he passed a newsstand? Or had he gotten used to her looks, the way others had? Lemon couldn't say he liked Edward, but there was just something so pitiful about him.

Lemon was feeling kindly and generous that day. He thought that maybe he could offer the poor boy a chance to impress his father today.

A smattering of unenthusiastic applause told him that Papa Vanderman had finished his announcement. Now he was calling for questions. Lemon's hand shot up.

"I have a question for Edward Vanderman Junior." Vanderman looked surprised, but he nodded at his son, who jumped up from his chair and joined his father at the microphone.

"Yes?" he asked.

Lemon winked at him surreptitiously. "It's my understanding that you are responsible for bringing Penelope Wilhern to the attention of the media and the public at large," he intoned solemnly. "And there are rumors that you may have had a relationship with the so-called pig-girl. Could you comment on this?"

"You know, I'm glad you asked that question," Edward said. "I'm furious, I'm outraged by the attention the media has given this—this creature. The woman is a freak, she's a monster, she belongs in a zoo! Putting her on your front pages—you're frightening small children!" He was getting so excited he didn't seem to notice the hostile rumble that was spreading through the room.

Lemon looked around at his colleagues and experienced some trepidation. They seemed to be taking Edward's criticisms very personally. Not that journalists were all that sensitive or susceptible to hurt feelings. They were reacting to Edward's comments the way parents would react if someone insulted their children. Didn't Edward have any idea how beloved Penelope had become? Couldn't he see the response he was provoking? Any minute now the reporters were going to start looking for things to throw at him.

Vanderman Senior sensed this, and he pushed his son away from the microphone. "Gentlemen, ladies, I'll now turn this over to the CEO of Clifton Enterprises." As another man rose from his seat, Vanderman gripped Edward's arm tightly and dragged him off the podium.

Another man stood at the microphone now and started to speak, but Lemon was getting out of the crowd of reporters. He made his way out of the room and ran down the corridor. Placing himself behind the elevator, he could hear every word exchanged between the Vandermans as they approached. He whipped out his notebook and started to write.

"Are you out of your mind?" the elder Vanderman snapped. "You can't talk about Penelope like that!"

"Father, I told you, she's a pig. She's disgusting. She's got a snout!"

"I don't care if she's got a curly tail and squeals *oink oink,* the people love her. Do you have any idea what kind of bad press you've just given us? We're a public company! We love what the people love!"

"But Father—"

Poor slob, Lemon thought as the elder Vanderman continued to berate his son loudly. Edward could learn a lesson from Penelope.

"Not to mention the fact that we need media support for this merger. This is worse than having a nervous breakdown in public! You're going to make up for this, you idiot. And you're going to do something fast."

"But what can I do?"

Lemon was writing furiously. But unfortunately for him, at that very moment, the elevator doors opened, the Vandermans stepped in, and it was left to Lemon's imagination to guess what Edward might possibly do to make up for his latest humiliation.

# Chapter Twenty-five

The pub was packed that evening, so maybe that's why I didn't see him right away. I was playing darts with Annie and a group of new friends, all Cloverdilly regulars.

Life was good. I was still pretty much doing the same things I'd always done—studying French, exercising, taking care of plants. But now my routine had a twist—I was taking French at a school, with other people, in a real class. I exercised at a health club. And I volunteered afternoons at the botanical gardens, showing visitors around and telling them about the plants.

The five-thousand-dollar reward I'd been paid for my photos was starting to run out, but I'd just picked up another fee for appearing in an advertisement for a candy company. Their latest product was chocolate truffles, and since real truffles were sniffed out by pigs, they thought it would be cute to have a pig-girl posing with their chocolate truffles. Any day now, pictures of me with chocolate smeared on my snout would be showing up in magazines. I didn't think they would be very flattering, but they'd keep me from having to hit up my parents for money.

Not that I'd written off my family. I still went back to the mansion on a regular basis, to tend my plants there, and I thought my mother was coming around to the fact that I was no longer in hiding. I'd been there just that morning, and I was surprised to see that the matchmaker was still hanging around.

"What's Wanda doing here?" I asked my mother.

"Penelope, despite what you've done, I haven't given up," my mother told me. "She's arranged for a suitor to come tonight."

My heart sank. "Tonight?"

My mother eyed me sternly. "You haven't forgotten that you're coming here for dinner tonight, have you?"

If only. "No, I haven't forgotten, but I thought it would be just us."

"You still want to get married, Penelope, don't you?"

"Well, sure, eventually. But I'm not in so much of a rush anymore."

My mother was shocked. "What do you mean, you're not in a rush anymore? Do you want to go on with that face? You *have* to get married, Penelope, that's the only way to lift the curse."

I sighed. "But Mom, things have changed for me. I'm happy now. I've got a life. I've got friends."

"Friends!" My mother shook her head. "You don't have friends, Penelope, you have *fans*. You're a fad.

You're the flavor of the week. This is not real popularity, any more than that face is your real face."

I was insulted. "Mother, how can you say that? Did it ever occur to you that maybe they *like* me?"

"How can they like you?" she countered. "They don't know you. Nobody knows *you,* they know a talking pig. All this fame and attention—I'm sorry, dear, but it won't last. People will get bored with you very soon."

I wanted to argue with her, but I wasn't sure how. I'd been so happy these past few weeks, I hadn't given much thought to the future. It was sort of like what Annie had advised—I wasn't thinking as much of who I would be someday. I was just being.

But maybe I was wrong, and maybe Annie didn't understand. My mother put her hands on my shoulders and forced me to face her directly. "Penelope, wouldn't you want your new friends to know the real you? Then you'd know which ones are really your friends."

I hated to admit it, but she had a point. And that was what I was thinking about as I took my turn throwing a dart at the Cloverdilly that evening.

"Yay, Penelope!" a chorus of voices greeted my very first bull's-eye.

"You go, girl!" Annie yelled. "Hey, where did I leave my beer?"

"I'll get it," I offered. I went over to the table where we'd left our drinks.

"Hello, Penelope."

I hadn't heard the voice in a while, but it still had the power to send shivers up my spine. I turned to face Max and the shivers turned into jolts of electricity. I'd forgotten how cute he was. No, that wasn't true, I hadn't forgotten at all—I'd just been trying very hard not to think about it.

"Hello, Max. How are you?"

"Fine. I guess I don't have to ask how *you're* doing. I can see how happy you are. Congratulations."

"For what?"

"For breaking out. Leaving home. That took guts. What made you do it?"

"I wanted to be free," I said.

There was no mistaking the fact that his eyes were shining in admiration. "Well, you're free now. Not just free, you're famous. How does that feel?"

I laughed, embarrassed, and studied the floor. "A little weird, I guess. But okay."

"I admire you," he said simply.

I looked up. "Do you, Max? Really? So, now that I'm famous, have you changed your mind? Do you want to marry me now?"

I'd intended that remark to sound like a wisecrack, nudge-nudge, wink-wink, a private joke. But it didn't come out that way. Even as the words came out of my mouth, I could hear how they sounded. It was a real request, and I wished desperately I could take it back. How pathetic could I be? Didn't I have any pride?

At least Max had the courtesy not to appear embarrassed by my outburst. He didn't even lose eye contact.

"I'm sorry, Penelope. I still can't."

"I was just kidding," I assured him hurriedly. "I've got to go. Nice seeing you."

I hurried back to Annie with her drink and realized she'd been watching me.

"So that's him."

I feigned innocence. "Him who?"

"The guy. The love of your life. The man you can't live without."

Forcing a smile, I shook my head. "No, I'm hoping that guy is going to be at my parents' tonight."

"Another blind date?"

I nodded.

Annie sighed. "Your mother never gives up, does she?"

"She can't," I replied. "And if I ever want to be myself, neither can I."


The words were still ringing in my ears as I entered the house a little while later.

"Hello, Jake. How's everything?"

"Just the same, Miss Penelope. Nothing ever changes."

"Oh, come on, that's not true, Jake!" I exclaimed. "Things change. Look at me!"

"You're still the same, miss."

It was an oddly personal thing for him to say, and I was annoyed. That was so not true! I'd left home. I was making a life for myself. I was famous. I was Penelope Pig!

"Your young man hasn't arrived yet, miss."

Then I realized what he meant when he said "Nothing changes." I was still cursed.

"Where's my mother?" I asked him.

"She's waiting for you in the dining room with Miss Wanda," Jake said.

They were huddled together whispering when I walked in, and they stopped the second they saw me. I looked at them with suspicion.

"What's going on?" I asked.

"Nothing," my mother said quickly. "We were just discussing the visitor who's coming to see you tonight."

"And just who is this visitor?" I asked. "I would have thought you'd run out of blue bloods by now."

Wanda bit her lip. "Well, this is someone who's had, well, let's just say he's had second thoughts. And he's coming back to see you."

My heart was in my throat. For one wild and crazy moment, I thought she might be talking about Max. "He . . . he's coming back?"

My mother rose. "And there he is!"

I turned to the window that displayed the music room.

And my heart, which was in my throat, sank to the pit of my stomach.

"Edward."

"Now, don't judge him by his earlier behavior," my mother pleaded. "Give him a chance to explain."

"Explain what? Why he ran away from me?"

"Yes, exactly!" she said brightly. "Now you go right in there and listen to what he has to say to you."

I groaned. "Can't I just listen to his apology through the window? I'm really not in the mood to hear him scream. Or watch him pass out, or throw up, or . . . *die*. Actually, maybe that wouldn't be so bad."

"Penelope! That's a terrible thing to say!"

"Yeah, you're right," I admitted. I looked through the window at Edward. He was pacing nervously. He actually *did* look like he might throw up any minute. I almost felt sorry for him.

"All right, Mother."

I went through the door into the music room. "Hello, Edward."

He turned to me, and I had to admire his control. His face was pale, but he didn't scream, and his lips formed a thin smile. "Hello, Penelope."

"Would you like to sit down?" I asked.

"Not exactly." And to my surprise, he knelt down on one knee.

"Edward, what are you doing?"

"Oh, Penelope, I've been such a fool. When I ran

away last time, I wasn't running away from you. I was running from my feelings. My feelings about you."

I looked at him blankly. "Huh?"

"I was afraid: afraid of the future, afraid of commitment. I was afraid to . . . to love."

I was completely bewildered. "To love who?"

"You, Penelope! I've always been in love with you, from our very first conversation. You captured my heart, you were the only person in the world who understood me."

I scratched my head. "I'm not sure I understand you all that well right this minute, Edward."

It was like he hadn't heard me. "I can't stop thinking about you. You're on my mind day and night. I dream of you. You're the only girl in the world for me."

That was when I realized he was holding a tiny box.

"Penelope . . . darling, wonderful Penelope . . ." He opened the box. The diamond was big enough to light up the room.

"Will you marry me?"

# Chapter Twenty-six

Lemon had begun to realize that moving up in the world of journalism left something to be desired—namely, excitement. He'd hoped that by this time he'd be hanging out at City Hall and exposing corrupt politicians, but instead he'd been promoted to assistant editor. So he sat at a desk all day and copyedited stories about corrupt politicians. He was beginning to look back with longing on the days when he talked to the victims of alien abductions.

So when the features editor appeared at his door, he looked up eagerly.

"I'm short on reporters today," the editor told him. "Want to go out on a human interest story?"

"Absolutely," Lemon said. "Anything, you name it."

"It's an interview. We're calling it 'from blue blood to jailbird.'"

"Who is he?"

"A fellow named Maxwell Campion. He's over at the county jail."

Lemon was stunned. "You're kidding. What happened? He passed a bad check?"

The editor shook his head. "Armed robbery."

Now Lemon was in complete shock. He couldn't believe it. Max may have had some attitude adjustment problems, sure, but he couldn't imagine the young man getting violent. "Are you sure? You didn't mix up the names?"

The editor glanced at the paper in his hand. "Nope, I've got the police report right here. So how about it, you want the assignment?"

"Yes."

Lemon liked to think that, over the years, he'd developed the objectivity all good journalists needed to have, and that he wouldn't ever let personal feelings come into his stories. But this wasn't going to be easy, interviewing Max, seeing a guy he'd become . . . well, almost fond of . . . behind bars. He could remember thinking that Max had a sensitive quality, that he showed some real decency in his personality, particularly when he refused to exploit Penelope by taking her picture. This was a real shocker.

And Lemon was equally surprised at himself. After all these years of meeting every kind of good, bad, and strange human being who existed, how could he have become such a poor judge of character?

What could have possibly driven Max to this? For a moment he felt guilty, wondering if Max's need for money had anything to do with the debt he'd been paying off to Lemon. But it was more likely that he'd just gone back to his old gambling habits and run out of money to put on the table.


Lemon had been to the jail before, of course, for his job. It wasn't one of his favorite places. As he turned his van off the road through the big gates, he could feel himself becoming depressed. Passing guards everywhere. Showing his identification every three steps. Feeling the angry, bitter eyes of prisoners in white jumpsuits and handcuffs.

From experience, he knew the procedure for interviewing a prisoner. He waited in a reception area with sad-faced wives and girlfriends, confused-looking children, and the occasional shady-looking colleague. When his name was called, he was escorted into another room made up of little desks in separated cubicles. There was a chair on either side of each desk, and the desks were divided by a glass wall. The glass dividers had a telephone on each side.

"Number four," the guard told him in a bored voice.

Lemon walked over to the booth and saw a heavyset man sitting and waiting on the other side of the glass. He went back to the guard. "No, my name's Lemon, I'm here to see Max Campion."

"Number *four*," the guard repeated.

He must have gone to the wrong booth. Lemon looked at the numbers carefully this time. But the booth labeled "four" was the same booth he'd already checked, and the same man was on the other side.

The prisoner picked up his phone and indicated that Lemon do the same.

"You the guy from the newspaper?"

"Y-yes, but I think there's been a mistake. I'm here to see Maxwell Campion."

"That's me, Max Campion."

"Then . . . there must be another Max Campion."

"Nah, I was an only child."

This is a bright one, Lemon thought. "No, I mean . . . someone else with the last name Campion and the first name Max."

The man looked completely blank.

"Maxwell Campion," Lemon said again. "The son of the late real estate mogul Clarence Campion."

"Hey, I know my old man's name. Just like I know mine. Now, you gonna interview me or what?"

It dawned on Lemon that there was something vaguely familiar about this guy. He tried to picture him in a loud, flowered Hawaiian shirt.

"You ever gamble in the back room of the Cloverdilly Pub?"

"Yeah, sure, what about it?"

It was like he was struck with lightning. No . . . more like he was nearsighted and had just put on corrective glasses. Suddenly everything was clear. The long-ago event went into instant mental replay.

The Cloverdilly Pub and a beefy-looking bouncer on a stool. Lemon asking him to point out Max Campion. The man indicated a table where a heavyset guy in a brightly flowered Hawaiian shirt, a blue-haired woman, an old man, and a younger one were playing cards.

"That's him."

The younger guy was getting up, so that was who Lemon thought the bouncer was referring to. He was wrong. He was supposed to be looking at the guy in the Hawaiian shirt.

It all made sense—the way Max didn't respond when Lemon first called out his name. He could still hear the conversation.

*"Listen, Campion, I got a proposition for you."*

*"You got the wrong guy."*

"Hey, reporter guy, you got questions for me or what?"

"Yeah, I've got a question," Lemon said. "When you were gambling at the Cloverdilly, there was a guy who was at your table a lot. Young guy, shaggy hair. You know his name?"

Campion scrunched his forehead. "Yeah, Marty."

"Marty what?"

"No, wait. Martin."

"Okay, Martin what?"

"Nah, it's what Martin."

"Huh?"

Campion snapped his fingers and looked immensely proud of himself. "Johnny! Johnny Martin."

Lemon jumped up. "Thanks, pal."

"That's it? You don't want to ask me any more questions?"

But Lemon was already leaving the room. He had another interview to prepare.

# *Chapter Twenty-seven*

I was alone in the dressing room, waiting in my underwear for the saleslady to bring me stuff to try on. All the women working in the store had twittered excitedly when I walked in. I assumed that in their line of business, they checked the society pages regularly, so they'd seen the announcement. It had appeared in every paper in town, and probably some out-of-town ones, too.

*Mr. and Mrs. Franklin Wilhern are pleased to announce the engagement of their daughter, Penelope, to Edward Vanderman Junior, son of Mr. and Mrs. Edward Vanderman Senior. The ceremony will take place at the Wilhern estate . . .*

Et cetera, et cetera.

I'd been surprised to see that my mother had settled for *pleased*—I'd expected something more like *ecstatic*.

"Now, what do you think of this, Miss Wilhern?" The woman carried the gown across two arms, like a long white baby. "It's classic, very traditional. Does that appeal to you?"

"I don't know," I said. "Maybe." I knew that most girls spent the weeks before their weddings thinking about their dresses and poring over pictures, and Annie had been bringing over stacks of bridal magazines, but every time I looked at them I started laughing. I wasn't sure why. Maybe because the image of a pig-bride was funny. Or maybe it was to keep from crying.

Obediently, I allowed the woman to help me into the white silk and fasten what felt like a thousand hooks. "Of course, it will need shortening, and taking in at the waist, but this should give you an idea." She turned me in the direction of the mirror.

I didn't laugh—I guess because I didn't look funny. It was a pretty dress, elegant and low-key. "Nice," I said.

The woman seemed disappointed. "Just nice? Oh, I think I understand. You want something more modern. I mean, you're not exactly a classic-type bride, are you?"

"No," I said. "Not exactly."

She helped me out of the gown, took it away, and returned with another bundle of white stuff. This turned out to be a long, narrow tube that stuck to every curve on my body.

"You look like a Grecian statue!" the woman cried in rapture.

"Are there many Greek statues of pigs?" I asked.

Now the woman uttered gales of laughter. "Oh, you are so cute!"

My mother was right—I was a novelty, the cute little talking pig. Well, not for much longer.

"Maybe it's a little too plain," the woman said. "Let me find something a little more fun." The dress came off, I waited, and another dress came in. This one looked like mounds and mounds of whipped cream.

"Penelope? Where are you?"

"In here, Annie."

Annie joined us in the dressing room. "Sorry I'm late. Did I miss anything wonderful?"

"Something classic and something simple. What do you think of this one?"

Annie gave the fluffy white clouds a once-over. "You look like something to eat."

I agreed. "That's what I thought. Pork in meringue. Yum."

The saleswoman went off into her hysteric giggles again. "She is so funny!" she said to Annie.

*She* was getting on my nerves. I told her to bring a selection of dresses, and my friend would help me get them on and off.

The next one was less fluffy, but too sparkly. "What do you think?" I asked Annie.

"It's not you," she said.

"Annie, *I'm* not me."

"Oh, come on, Penelope, how can you say that?"

"Because it's true! This isn't my face, it's my great-great-great-grandfather's face." I grinned. "It's ironic, in a way. I won't know if I'm wearing a dress that's right for me until after I say 'I do.' "

"What's it like living back at home?"

I'd just moved back that morning. With all the fuss involved in preparing for the wedding, I'd let myself be talked into it.

"Not too bad. My mother's in an excellent mood, surprise, surprise."

Annie smiled, but I could see there was something else on her mind.

"Penelope . . ."

"What?"

"Do you love him?"

I tried on the veil that came with the dress. "I wonder if I should keep this over my face through the ceremony. Then, after we're pronounced husband and wife, I'll lift it and—voilà! Do you think that would be too theatrical?"

"Penelope, you didn't answer my question. Do you love Edward Vanderman?"

"Edward Vanderman Junior," I corrected her. "You know, Annie, I think that he's basically a decent person. It's just that he's an only child and he was very spoiled by his parents. Particularly his mother; she still treats him like a baby. He's got some growing up to do."

"But do you love him?" Annie persisted.

"In his own way, he *is* kind of lovable," I told her. "He's just got a lack of confidence. And a big ego. Wait, is that a contradiction in terms?"

"Penelope!"

I sighed, and took off the veil. "He can break the curse, Annie. That's what matters."

"But what about that guy at the Cloverdilly? The way you were looking at him, I know you've got feelings for him. Can't he break the curse?"

I smiled sadly. "He doesn't want to. Annie, try to understand. All my life, I've been wearing a face that isn't mine. I want to be me."

Annie gave me a quick hug. "I know, I understand. Okay, maybe Edward isn't the man of your dreams. But if you want to marry him . . . well, I'll be there to celebrate with you."

"Thanks," I said. "And who knows? Maybe I can learn to love Edward."

Annie looked doubtful. "You really think so?"

I considered the possibility. "Well . . . I can learn to tolerate him."

"What would happen if you married him and then divorced him?" Annie wanted to know. "Would your snout grow back?"

"I don't think I'll want to find out," I said. "Okay, what about this gown?"

We finally agreed on one, and the saleswoman came in to measure me and stick pins in it for alterations.

Afterward, we went to the florist's across the street to look at flowers for my bouquet.

"Penelope, look! Yellow tulips, your favorite!"

They were gorgeous. I oohed and ahhed over the tubs filled with huge, shiny, bright yellow flowers. There wasn't a flower in the world that could make me happier.

"She's getting married," Annie told the shopkeeper.

"Are you interested in a wedding bouquet made up of yellow tulips?" the man asked me.

But strangely enough, the thought of carrying yellow tulips to marry Edward didn't fill me with happiness. Or maybe it wasn't just the flowers that didn't seem right.


The minute the lights came down in the concert hall, Edward's eyelids went down, too. I just hoped he wouldn't snore.

He hadn't been thrilled about this family evening out, but the two sets of parents had been insistent. It was a benefit concert, raising money for some chic cause; I didn't even know what it was. But Vanderman Industries or Enterprises or whatever it was called was one of the sponsors, so Edward's family had to be there. And since it was going to be a very fashionable event, my mother wanted to go, too.

Not just for the music, either. She and my father hadn't been out much in the past twenty-five years. My condition had turned them into hermits, too. Now that everyone knew about me, they could socialize again. In a way, my fame had freed the whole family. My mother didn't even try to make me wear a vintage hat with a little veil.

It was a jazzy orchestra, and I liked the music. It was the first time I'd heard live music like this, and I was carried away with the sound. When Edward's mother passed me her little binoculars, I didn't really want them—it was nice just listening, I didn't need to see the musicians' faces. But she'd offered them, so I took them to be nice. Holding them to my eyes, I surveyed the faces of the musicians. It was sort of interesting, seeing the different expressions. Some of them looked intense, like they were concentrating; some of them looked dreamy, like they were into the sounds. . . .

And one of them looked like Max Campion.

I leaned forward, gripping the binoculars tightly. It *was* Max, bent over the piano keyboard, his hands pounding the keys.

I opened the program, and searched for his name, but it wasn't there. The pianist was listed as "Johnny Martin." Max must have been substituting for him.

I was glad Edward was sleeping. It had to be showing on my face, the way I was feeling. Edward probably wouldn't be able to recognize the expression, but I still didn't want him to see it. He might remember how I looked, and wonder why I never looked at him like this.

When the concert was over, there was a party for the sponsors of the concert and the band. I considered developing a massive headache, but found myself dragged along with the family to the reception hall. At least it was big, and crowded, so there was a good chance I wouldn't run into Max.

So why did I go looking for him? Using the usual restroom excuses, I extracted myself from the little family group and wandered off alone.

Moving through the crowd, I saw a lot of musicians, but not the one I wanted to see. I wondered if maybe Max had skipped out on the party. I didn't think he was a party type, and besides, he'd been a substitute, not a regular member of the orchestra, so maybe he didn't feel like he needed to attend. However, I did locate a buffet with some mini-éclairs, and collected a few in a napkin. Since I didn't like to eat in public—I always had to be on guard for pigging-out jokes—I took my little treasure trove into what appeared to be some kind of lounge.

I didn't make it past the door frame. There were two people already in there, and I immediately recognized their voices.

"Don't do it, Vanderman. It's not right. You're not doing it for her, you're not even doing it for yourself. You're doing it to make your old man happy."

"My father's making me a vice president. What do you think of that?"

"I think you're just desperate for his respect. Is that worth ruining Penelope's life?"

"You had your chance, Campion. You didn't want her. This is none of your business."

Nothing that had been said came as news to me. I knew why Edward was marrying me. I knew why I was marrying Edward. We were both using each other to get what we wanted.

There was one element that surprised me, though. How did Edward know Max? Maybe there were blue-blood clubs for guys.

"Something else I don't get, Campion. Why do you care if I marry Penelope? What's it to you?"

*This* intrigued me. I strained to hear Max's response.

"I care because you don't love her, Vanderman. You made that loud and clear. What was it you called her— a monster? You couldn't bear the sight of her! Why did you change your mind?"

"I didn't," Edward snapped. "But do you want to tell her I'm completely grossed out by the very thought of having to kiss her? You want to break the pig's heart?"

I edged back out of the doorway and dropped my éclairs into a wastebasket. Slowly, I made my way back to the reception hall.

My father spotted me and came over. "Are you all right, Penelope?"

"Fine, Dad," I replied automatically.

"You're sure?" He put an arm around me. "You don't look happy. Is it . . . is it Edward?"

I didn't say anything.

"You know, darling, despite what your mother says . . . you don't *have* to marry him."

I touched the face that wasn't really mine.

"Yes, Dad. I do."

# Chapter Twenty-eight

Armed with a folder filled with Internet printouts, Lemon strode into the Cloverdilly the next morning. There were no customers in there yet, only the cleaning guy.

"How ya doing, Johnny Martin?"

The young man formerly-known-as-Max continued to sweep, but he looked up just long enough to flash an abashed grin. "Took you long enough to figure it out, Lemon. Not much of an investigative journalist, are you?"

"Hey, I've been covering UFO sightings and two-headed alligators," Lemon replied. "The only investigating I've done has been my search for Penelope Wilhern. And that only took twenty-five years."

The young man grimaced. "But you caught up with her in the end."

"Yeah, and it's on my conscience," Lemon said.

"Well, maybe you did her a good deed in the long run. You got her out of that house."

Lemon nodded. "Yeah, and now someone's finally willing to marry her and break the spell. Unfortunately, that someone is Edward Vanderman Junior. What do you think of that, Mr. Martin?"

"Just call me Johnny, okay?" He leaned the broom against the wall, and sat down on the piano stool. With one hand, he picked out some notes on the keys.

Lemon didn't know much about music, but instinctively he realized the guy had talent. With just a little tune, he could demonstrate how he felt, what he thought about the upcoming marriage of Penelope and Vanderman.

"You care about her, don't you?" Lemon asked.

Johnny continued playing. He didn't answer Lemon's question, but he didn't have to. It was all in the music.

Lemon interpreted what he was hearing. "You love her," he stated flatly.

Johnny took his hands off the keys and slammed down the lid. Rising, he grabbed his broom and began sweeping furiously.

"I wondered about that," Lemon went on. "I knew there was something going on, the first time you went to meet her and you didn't take a picture. At first I thought you just felt sorry for her, but the longer it went on, the more I got the idea you were feeling something stronger."

Silently, Johnny pushed the grime from the floor onto a tray and emptied the tray into a wastebasket. Then he picked up a rag and started to wipe down the bar.

Lemon continued. "And I started thinking, this doesn't make sense. If he's in love with her, why doesn't he want to marry her and break the spell? That's when I went online and did a little work."

He indicated the folder he had in his hand. "Now, I'm not a techie and this is all pretty new to me. But it's amazing what you can dig up about people on Google."

Johnny spoke. "Even about nobodies like me?"

Lemon sat down at a table and opened his folder. "John Andrew Martin," he read. "Age twenty-five. Studied piano, played with the New Age Jazz Band. Let go after four months. Played with the Lloyd Dirkson Band. Let go after six weeks. Piano man for the Cloverdilly Bar."

Johnny finished his own resume. "Three weeks. Fired."

"What's the matter, are you a lousy piano player?" Lemon asked.

"No, I'm good, damned good," Johnny said. "But I had a little problem." He paused. "A big problem."

Lemon didn't have to guess what it was. "Gambling."

Johnny's face was grim. "Couldn't stay away from the tables. Day and night. I missed a lot of rehearsals. Half the time I didn't show up for shows, and the other half I was too exhausted to play well. And I was broke. I got evicted from my apartment last month."

"Things getting better for you?"

Johnny nodded. "Gamblers Anonymous. Haven't had

a card in my hand for three months." He actually smiled. "And I've started playing again, with a new jazz band. Maybe one of these days I'll be able to afford a place to live."

"Where are you staying now?"

Johnny opened a door. On the floor of the storage room lay a mattress.

Lemon grimaced. "Oh man, that's sad." Then, impulsively, he said, "I've got a spare room at my place you could have."

"Yeah?

"Until you're back on your feet, financially."

"Wow." Johnny looked eternally grateful. "That would be great. It wouldn't be forever, it looks like I'll start making some money. I think this new band's gonna do well. We had a gig last night at the concert hall, big society benefit." Then the grim expression returned to his face. "I saw Penelope there with the Vandermans." He slammed his fist on the bar.

"Hey, be careful!" Lemon yelped. "You make your living with those hands. I don't want you shacking up with me forever."

"Yeah, I know. But I just get so . . . *mad*. I tried to talk to Edward last night. I was hoping maybe he'd changed. But he doesn't give a damn about her. He's just following Daddy's orders."

"I know," Lemon said. "So how can you let this happen?"

Johnny gazed at him evenly. "If you've done your research properly, you know why."

Lemon nodded and returned to his notes. "Son of Eric Martin," he read. He paused and looked up. "Plumber."

"He's a damned good one, too," Johnny said. "But you know the curse. Only one of her own kind can lift it."

"And you're no blue blood."

"Exactly."

Lemon studied him thoughtfully. "But you love her."

"So what? Didn't you hear what I said? I can't lift the curse."

"But you love her!" Lemon said again. "Maybe that's more important to her."

"More important than becoming normal after twenty-five years?" Johnny was incredulous. "Are you nuts?"

"How do you know what she thinks? Have you ever considered telling her that you love her?"

"No. And I never will."

"But why not? Don't you think she deserves to know?"

"I think she deserves to have a normal life," Johnny snapped.

"But maybe she'd rather have *you!* I think maybe she loves you."

Johnny's face was crossed with pain. "That's what I'm afraid of."

"Hold on, wait a minute," Lemon said. "I'm not following you."

"I'm afraid she'd give up her chance to be normal, for me."

"Isn't that her choice to make?" Lemon asked.

"I don't even want to tempt her. She deserves a crack at happiness." The pain on his face was almost unbearable to watch, and Lemon looked away.

"I won't take that chance away from her," Johnny said quietly.

Back in his van, Lemon pounded his steering wheel in frustration. Why, why, why had he let himself get so involved? All he'd wanted was a photo and a story. Why did he care what happened to the pig-girl? Or Johnny, for that matter?

He shook his head wearily. Maybe he *was* a decent guy after all. And now he couldn't change back. In grim determination, he started the van and took off.

His old parking space in front of the Wilhern mansion was available. Was that a good omen or a bad one? Either way, he knew this wasn't going to be easy.

The butler opened the door. He took one look at Lemon and started to close it. Lemon stuck his foot in the door frame.

"Ow!" he yelped as the butler continued to push on the door. "Wait, man! This is about Penelope. Do you care about her at all?"

"Excuse me, sir?"

"I'll bet you do, and so do I. And I've got some information here that just might change her life."

The butler's face was implacable, though there seemed to be something going on behind his eyes. He actually opened the door and let Lemon in. "Please wait in the music room. I will see if Miss Penelope is available."

Lemon tried not to think about the last time he was in this house. He only had one good eye left and he intended to keep it. With that one eye, he gazed around the room. Pretty ritzy joint, these Wilherns had. He went over to the mirror to check himself and make sure he was presentable.

He'd barely had a glimpse of his reflection before he heard the scream. Seconds later, the door to the music room flew open and Jessica Wilhern burst in. Lemon shrank against the wall in fear.

"WHAT ARE YOU DOING IN MY HOUSE?"

He had a feeling she'd now destroyed one of his ears. And her call brought support in the form of Franklin Wilhern and another woman.

"I need to see Penelope," Lemon managed to squeak.

"OVER MY DEAD BODY!"

At least the husband seemed to embody an element of humanity. "Why do you need to see Penelope?"

"I have to tell her about Johnny Martin."

"WHO THE HELL IS JOHNNY MARTIN?"

"I think she knows him as Max Campion."

The shriek that greeted this announcement did serious damage to the other ear. "DON'T SAY THAT NAME IN THIS HOUSE!"

"Calm down, dear," Franklin Wilhern urged. "Wanda, wasn't Max Campion the young man who visited several times?"

"Yes," the other woman said. "Three times. He refused to marry Penelope."

"But he had a reason," Lemon said. He explained what he'd learned about Johnny, and he showed them what he had in his folder.

Wanda sighed. "So he was just pretending to be Maxwell Campion. He can't lift the curse."

Lemon nodded. "Johnny Martin is not a blue blood. But . . ." He took a deep breath. "He's in love with her."

The silence in the room was heavenly. It didn't last.

"SO WHAT?"

But Franklin Wilhern and Wanda actually seemed intrigued. "Really?" Wanda asked. "He loves her?"

And Franklin's eyes seemed to mist over. "We must get Penelope. She should know this."

Lemon nodded. "That's what I thought."

But Jessica Wilhern didn't share their opinion. "NO!"

Franklin was clearly surprised. "What are you saying, my dear?"

Jessica Wilhern was calmer now, but no less determined. "I do not want Penelope to know about this

Max-Johnny person, whoever he is. If he can't lift the curse, he can't marry her."

"But don't you think that's Penelope's decision to make?" Wanda asked.

"NO! HE CAN'T BREAK THE CURSE! Jake! Jake! Where *is* he? Oh, it doesn't matter. I'll throw him out myself."

Now it was Lemon's turn to shriek and run. And he managed to get himself out of the room before she could get anywhere near his good eye.

# *Chapter Twenty-nine*

I opened my bedroom window and stuck my head out. It was a gorgeous day, one of the earliest days of summer. There were no clouds in the brilliantly aqua blue sky. The sun was bright, and warm, but it wasn't sweltering hot outside. I'd read about days like this in books. Writers could get very poetic when they described days like this. With the right words, they could make you hear bluebirds, feel the warmth of the sun, smell the faint sweetness of the honeysuckle and the newly mown lawns. I used to wonder if I'd ever experience a day like this in my real life.

And here it was, finally, a day just like the writers described. A day that I could actually appreciate, and in person. A perfect day for a wedding.

I checked out the scene from another window. This one looked directly down onto the grounds where the ceremony would take place. It was only eight in the morning—the ceremony wouldn't start until seven in the evening—but people were already hard at work getting things organized. Rows and rows of white chairs had already been set up. My mother had invited everyone who was anyone. Plus my friends. Annie, of course, the bartender, and some of the regulars from the Cloverdilly. That was the only real request I'd made in regard to the wedding.

I'd pretty much left the whole business in my mother's hands, and I didn't have to feel guilty about that because I knew she'd enjoyed every minute of it. Every now and then she would demand my opinion about something, or ask me to make a choice—pink, peach, or lavender? Shrimp or crab? To get her off my back, I'd choose one, knowing full well she would automatically decide on the other. It didn't really matter to me.

For me, the great significant event of the day would come after the ceremony, and it wasn't the reception I was thinking about, either.

I took my secret mirror, the compact that I'd stolen long ago from my mother's handbag, and looked in it. Holding it with one hand, I put the other over my snout. Of course, I'd done this a zillion times, but this time I was trying very hard to get a real sense of what I was going to look like in just a little while.

I remembered when Annie told me about her girl-friend who had a nose job. Annie said that when the bandages came off, the girl looked completely different, as if more than her nose had been changed. Would my face be completely different? It didn't really matter to me. However it looked, at least it would finally be *my* face.

There was a rap on my door, and as usual, my mother walked in before I had a chance to invite her. "What are you doing?" she asked.

"I was just wondering if I'm going to miss my old face," I said.

As always, she didn't pass up an opportunity to recite her mantra. "It's not your face, it's never been your face, it's your great-great-great-grandfather's face. Today, my darling, we will all finally see your real face."

I looked at her thoughtfully. "What if it's worse than this one?"

"Don't talk nonsense," she snapped. "We've got too much to do today. The beautician is coming to do your hair and your nails and your makeup. The seamstress will be here while you put on your gown, just in case she needs to make any last-minute alterations to the dress. Then you'll meet with the photographer. . . ."

I was surprised. "Before the ceremony? I thought you'd want to wait until I had my own face."

"Your face, I mean, your great-great-great-grandfather's face, will be covered with the veil," she assured me. "By the way, did I tell you I had a double lining sewn inside the veil? I was afraid the lace alone might be see-through."

I rolled my eyes in exasperation. "Mother! My picture's been in newspapers and magazines. Everyone's already seen my—*this*—face a thousand times. They all know what I look like."

"Memories are short," my mother said firmly. "Once everyone sees the real you at the reception, they'll forget all about the pig-girl."

She could be right, I supposed. I was suddenly glad I'd kept a scrapbook of my time as a celebrity. For some reason, *I* didn't want to forget.

The day passed quickly, with all my beauty treatments and pampering. I was coiffed and made up and dressed long before necessary. So I was pleased when Annie arrived early and came up to my room to see me.

We embraced, and Annie admired my dress, my hair, my jewelry, every detail down to my pedicure.

"You look fabulous!" she exclaimed, and I knew she meant it. But I could tell from her expression that there was something else she wanted to say.

"Talk," I commanded her. "Because my mother will be coming up here soon and then you'll never get a word in edgewise."

Annie hesitated.

I tried to help her out. "I know you don't like Edward. But maybe he'll grow on you. Better yet, maybe he'll grow on me."

Annie smiled. "Look, I know why you're marrying him. And I know how much it means to you, and I'm not going to try to talk you out of it. There's just one thing I wanted to say."

"Congratulations?"

"Well, that, too. But Penelope . . . you'll still be you, you know."

I looked at her in disbelief. "You don't think marrying Edward will lift the curse?"

She shrugged impatiently. "Okay, maybe you won't have a snout anymore. But it doesn't matter if you shave your head or cut off your ears or grow a third eye. You don't have to get married, not to Edward, not to anyone. With or without a snout, you'll still be you. And as far as I'm concerned, that's a good thing."

I didn't know what to say. Annie came over and kissed me on the cheek. "I'm going to grab a seat," she said. "I want to be in a good spot to catch the magic moment. I've never seen a nose fall off before."

The next time I looked out the window, the arrangements were complete. Having been unable to choose between peach, pink, and lavender, my mother had gone for an all-white theme. The white chairs were now adorned with white satin ribbons and drapes of white silk. At the end of each row was a huge ornamental display of white lilies in white organza, and the aisle I would walk down was strewn with the petals of a hundred white roses.

The vows would be taken under a bower of white lace held up by white alabaster pillars. Edward would wear a white suit. My mother had requested—that is, demanded—that all guests wear black, and I wouldn't put it past her to throw out anyone who showed up in navy blue. She'd hired public relations people to bring in all the people the Wilherns had been hiding from for so long—press, television, magazine people. She wanted to make up for twenty-five years of social hibernation.

She came in my room, carrying a large wrapped package in her arms. "Oh, Penelope. You look beautiful. I mean, you *will* look beautiful."

How could a person respond to a compliment like that? Should I tell her I would thank her in the near future when it was true?

"And just look at what I've brought you." She set the package down on my desk and ripped off the brown paper wrapping. It was a mirror.

"You can come right back up here after the ceremony and get a good look at yourself before the reception!"

"Would you mind if I look at myself right now?" I asked.

"Why would you want to do that?" she asked, but she stepped aside to give me space. I posed in front of the mirror, and I had to admit, I wasn't unhappy with the reflection. Somehow, despite my lack of interest, I'd managed to pick the right dress. The pearl jewelry I wore made my skin glow. My hair was perfect, the shiny dark brown curls cascading to my shoulders.

I tore myself from the mirror and went to the window. My mother joined me there, and we looked at the

setting for the wedding. "Isn't it glorious?" she en-
thused. "You're going to have the wedding of a princess,
my darling. And once it's over, you'll look like a
princess!"

I wished her enthusiasm was contagious.

I could see guests arriving and taking their seats.
Most of them were utter strangers to me, people my
parents had known before I was born. I did spot Annie
and the gang from the Cloverdilly.

But not Max. I'd lifted an invitation from my
mother's stack, I'd looked up his address in the phone
book, and I'd given it to Jake to mail. There had been
no reply. Still, I could always hope . . .

My mother finally left, to take her place in the front
row, and my father appeared at my door to escort me
outside and walk me down the aisle.

"Just a second, let me put on my veil," I said. I fastened the heavily lined headpiece to my hair, and realized that it was so thick I couldn't see through it.

"This is ridiculous," I fumed. I found a scissors and
cut two tiny holes in the cloth for my eyes. Only a person who got very, very close to me would confuse me
with Casper the ghost.

I took my father's arm, and he led me downstairs.
"Penelope . . . ," he began, then stopped.

"What is it, Dad?"

"I just want to tell you how very, very sorry I am."

"For what?"

"For your face! For the way you've had to grow up, alone, hidden away. I'm so sorry."

"Dad, there's nothing to be sorry for."

"Oh yes, there is," he insisted. "Because of my family, you haven't had a normal life. It's the Wilherns who have made you suffer."

"Oh, Dad, just let it go. I'm not suffering anymore."

I really wasn't suffering. We were coming down the aisle now, and I had spotted my friends. It dawned on me that I hadn't suffered for quite a while now.

Edward was waiting under the arbor. His expression was familiar—once again, he looked like he was about to throw up. He was probably thinking about the fact that he'd be expected to kiss me after we were pronounced husband and wife. I wished I could communicate to him that it wouldn't be any more pleasant for me than it would be for him. However, I knew that *I* would have the self-control to keep from vomiting. I wasn't so sure about him.

As we approached the judge who would be conducting the ceremony, I found that I was grateful for the ridiculously thick veil that covered my face. Not because I wanted to hide my snout. I was more concerned with hiding my expression. I had a feeling I didn't look very much like a bride was expected to look on her wedding day.

My father left me at Edward's side, and we faced the judge.

"Dearly beloved, we are gathered here to join this man and this woman . . ."

Out of the corner of my eye, thanks to the hole in the veil, I caught a glimpse of my mother. She was clearly ecstatic, and for the first time, I really understood why. This was more her day than mine.

I also saw Annie. She was smiling, too, but in a different way, like she was forcing herself to smile. Her forehead was puckered, as if she was worrying at the same time.

The judge had reached the point in the service that usually provided the high moment of drama in every soap opera I'd ever watched. "If there are any among us who object to this marriage, let them speak now or forever hold their peace."

I had a brief moment of fantasy—Max, rising from the audience, shouting "I object!" But the judge's words were greeted with the usual silence. This was real life, not a soap opera. Not a fairy tale.

"Edward Vanderman Junior, do you take this woman, Penelope Wilhern, as your lawful wedded wife? Do you promise to love and cherish her, in sickness and in health, for richer and for poorer, forsaking all others, till death do you part?"

I wouldn't say his response was wildly enthusiastic, but he did manage to squeak out an audible "I do."

"And do you, Penelope Wilhern, take this man, Edward Vanderman Junior, as your lawful wedded husband? Do you promise to love and cherish him, in sickness and in health, for richer and for poorer, forsaking all others, till death do you part?"

I'd always heard that right before you die, your entire life flashes right before your eyes. I didn't know it happened when you got married, too. But I saw it all, rushing before me, fast but clear. The lonely childhood. Someday your prince will come. That's not your face, Penelope. Walking through the park for the first time at night . . . and the recent times. Good times, with friends, having fun, talking, laughing, sharing thoughts and feelings.

I had a life now. And suddenly, I knew what I had to say. And I had to say it fast before I could have second thoughts.

"No. I don't."

# Chapter Thirty

I knew that my mother would be hot on my heels as I ran back up the aisle. Halfway back to the house, the veil on my head shifted and I couldn't see out of the holes I'd made, so I pulled the whole headdress off and tossed it. That was when I knew she was close—her shriek seemed almost as loud as the one she'd bellowed when I'd said no.

It wasn't like I could avoid her tirade forever, and I really didn't want to give her a heart attack, so I let her catch up once I was inside the house. She was on the step behind me as I started up the stairs.

"Penelope! What are you doing? Get back out there right this minute!"

"No, Mother. I'm not going to marry Edward."

"Are you crazy? What is this, last-minute jitters? It's all right, it's not too late, people will understand. I'll explain to them. Of course, you'll have to apologize to Edward. Or I could apologize for you. Penelope! Are you listening?"

"I'm listening, Mother. But I'm still not going to marry Edward. I don't love him, Mother. I don't even *like* him." I'd reached my bedroom by now. "And I'd like to be alone for a while."

I closed the bedroom door, but that didn't stop her from standing on the other side and talking through it.

"Penelope, this is insane! This is your chance, your one and only chance. This is what we've been waiting for, hoping for!"

"What *you've* been hoping for, Mother."

"What are you saying? You don't want to be happy?"

"Go away, Mother, *please*."

"All you have to say is 'I do' and you can have your own face! You can be yourself!"

Why couldn't she understand? Maybe because now *I* was just beginning to understand. "I'm myself right now, Mother! I don't need a different face to be happy, I'm happy now, even with this face. I like myself, just the way I am!"

I wanted to go on, to try to explain, but suddenly I couldn't speak. What was that feeling rushing through me? My whole body was throbbing, tingling, and my head was burning. I was spinning, the room was spinning, my whole world was spinning. And then I hit the floor.

"Penelope? Penelope! What was the noise? Are you all right?"

Lying flat on my back, I didn't know what to say. Nothing hurt. But something was different.

The bedroom door opened and Jessica came in. "Penelope?"

"I'm here, Mother."

She looked down and her expression froze. And for the first time ever, so did her mouth. It was open, but no sounds were coming out.

And then I knew why she was silent. I didn't know how I knew, but I knew. I put my hand to my face. Then I got up off the floor and went over to the mirror my mother had brought into my room earlier that day.

I knew what I'd see before I saw it. Me, Penelope Wilhern, of course. In a long, white wedding gown. With shiny dark brown curls cascading to her shoulders, with big brown eyes.

And with a perfect little normal nose.

# Chapter Thirty-one

My mother was crying again. Not shrieking, not screaming, not throwing one of her usual fits of frustration and despair. She was crying.

It had been going on like this for the past couple of hours. You'd think she'd be ecstatic, laughing, dancing for joy, celebrating my new face. I was still upstairs in my bedroom, and she was downstairs with my father and Wanda and Jake, but her hysterical wailing was as loud as every other sound that could come out of her mouth, and I could even make out the words she spoke between the sobs.

"I didn't know, I didn't know! How could I have known? 'One of our own kind,' that was what the curse said. Someone who would love her. I thought that meant a husband! Didn't you? Isn't that what you thought, too?"

I couldn't hear the normal voices of the people around her, but I assumed they were all agreeing with her. I agreed with her—that's what I'd thought, too.

Someone had to love and accept me just the way I was, snout and all. How could I have known that the someone could be me?

And would it have made any difference if I *had* known? How could I ever have loved myself when I was brought up to believe that I *wasn't* myself?

While she was crying, I was packing. I still had my little furnished room in Midtown, it was paid up till the end of the month, and I was going back there. I needed some time on my own, and I knew I wouldn't get that here. It was ironic—I'd spent most of my life so far alone, in hiding. Now that I didn't need to hide, I still wanted to be alone. Not forever, of course. But there was a lot I needed to think about, stuff I had to figure out for myself. And not because I was finally myself. I knew now that I'd been myself all the time.

I closed my suitcase and went over to the window. The catering company was still cleaning up, carrying away the chairs, taking down the reception tent. The guests were long gone, even Edward and his parents. I had a pretty good suspicion *he* was celebrating.

I picked up the suitcase and carried it downstairs. My parents were now alone in the music room.

"Where are you going?" Jessica shrieked when she saw me with the suitcase.

"Just back to my own place," I assured her. "Not far. I'll be back to visit."

My father nodded understandingly, but my mother

buried her face in her hands and let out a fresh onslaught of tears and wailing. "Oh, my darling, I'm sorry," she wept. "Can you ever forgive me? I'm so very, very sorry."

I was used to hearing my father say he was sorry, for being a Wilhern and therefore responsible for the curse. I'd never heard my mother apologize for anything before.

"Sorry for what?" I asked.

She wiped her eyes. "If only I'd done my job as a mother, if only I could have loved you just as you were, as one of my own, like a real mother should, the curse would have been lifted long ago."

What could I say? *It's okay, Mom, I don't blame you for being a shallow, superficial snob who couldn't bear the thought of anyone knowing she had an ugly child?* What would be the point? She was who she was. So I put down the suitcase and went to her. I put one arm around her, the other around my father, and we had a group hug.

Finally, my mother started to calm down. She turned to me, smiled, and studied my face.

"You know, dear, I just had a thought."

"What's that, Mom?"

"I'm presuming that the carotid artery is out of the way now. You could have some more work done on your nose! I think you'd be adorable with just a little turned-up tip . . . and maybe you could have your cheekbones lifted. . . ."

"Mother!" I pulled away and stared at her in aston-
ishment.

Her face was all innocence. "What's wrong with
wanting to look your best?"

I shook my head wearily. Like me, she would never
change, either.

Rising, I gave my father one more hug. "I'm going
now." They followed me out of the room and into the
entrance hall by the door. But before I could open it
and walk out, someone else came along with a suitcase
in hand.

"You won't be needing my services anymore, Ms.
Wilhern," Wanda said. "Penelope is perfectly capable of
finding a husband now on her own. If she wants one."
To me, she said, "Personally, if I were you, I'd have
some fun first. You've got a lot of time to make up for."
Bidding us all farewell, she walked out the door.

"Bye, Mom, Dad. I'll call you," I said, but once
again, someone beat me to the door.

"Jake!" my mother yelled. "What are you doing?"

He, too, was carrying a suitcase in one hand and an
old-fashioned walking stick in the other. Without saying a word, he nodded at my mother, my father, and
me. Then he opened the door and walked outside.

Jessica ran after him. My father and I followed them
outside.

"Jake!" my mother bellowed. "Where do you think
you're going? You can't quit! You come back here, right

this minute!" As he continued to walk toward the gate, her voice rose to an earth-shattering shriek. "Do you hear me? I said, come back here—"

She wasn't able to finish the sentence. Jake turned around, lifted his walking stick, and pointed it straight at her. My mother went completely dumb. Jake turned back and continued toward the gate.

My father and I watched Jessica in fascination. Her lips were moving, but nothing was coming out. She kept trying, she opened her mouth wider and wider, she took deep breaths as if she was trying to blow out the words— but there was nothing. She was mute.

I looked at my father, expecting him to look as upset as she did. But his expression was thoughtful. And as he put an arm around her to comfort her, I could have sworn I saw a small smile on his face.

I waved to them and walked down to the gate. As I emerged onto the sidewalk, I caught a glimpse of Jake just ahead of me.

"Good-bye, Jake," I called to him.

He turned, raising his stick in salute. And then he began to change. Right before my eyes, his body transformed, and our old butler was no longer standing straight and tall. His back curved and he was bent over. His formal butler suit seemed to melt away and was replaced by a ragged long dress. His hair turned gray and grew, long and wild until it hung to his waist. And his face—well, he certainly wasn't Jake. He was a woman, an ugly woman, with a pimply nose and a jutting chin. Even the walking stick had changed. It was longer, rougher, and crooked. Like something a witch might carry.

Then I knew. All this time, all these years, Jake had stayed with us in order to witness the vengeance. He was Clara-the-servant-girl's mother. And she'd settled her score with the Wilherns.

# Chapter Thirty-two

I arrived at my shop in the morning and paused outside to examine the display I'd created for the window.
It hadn't been easy, coming up with something creative
and attractive for Halloween, even though it was my
all-time favorite celebration. The holiday wasn't really
associated with flowers, and I certainly hadn't wanted
to do the standard ghosts and spiderweb thing, which
might indicate the season but had nothing at all to do
with what I sold in my shop.

Looking in the window now, I was actually proud of
what I'd managed to come up with: hollowed-out pump-
kins filled with tall tiger lilies and black hanging baskets
of orange spray roses and alstroemeria. It was festive
and seasonally correct, and not just for decoration—the
arrangements could be purchased inside, at Penelope's
Petals.

I unlocked the door, turned the CLOSED sign to OPEN,
took off my coat, and put it away. Then I filled a can
and watered all my plants. I went through the mail—just

bills and catalogs—and checked on the arrangements I needed to complete that day.

I was reading an interesting article about gerbera daisies when the tinkling of a bell indicated that the door to my shop had opened. A rush of cool, brisk autumn air came in with the customer.

I recognized the woman immediately. "Ms. Duquesne! Nice to see you. How was your honeymoon?"

"Glorious," the woman said. "Bermuda is beautiful at this time of year. When you plan your honeymoon, you should keep Bermuda in mind."

I smiled. "I don't believe I'll be planning my honeymoon any time soon. I thought it might be a good idea to find a husband first."

"Well, a beautiful young woman like you must have hundreds of men chasing you. Or hundreds of women, if you happen to be of that persuasion. Anyway, I just wanted to stop by and thank you again for the beautiful job you did on my wedding. People are still talking about the centerpieces on the tables. And you know, I refused to throw my bouquet in the traditional manner, it was just too magnificent. I'm having it pressed and framed."

"I'm glad you were pleased," I said.

"And I brought you some photos," the woman continued. "You could use them for advertising if you like. Or put them up here in the shop."

I accepted the pictures with appreciation. The shop had only been open for a month, and I needed all the publicity I could get. Besides, the Duquesne wedding had been my first really big job, and it was nice to have something to remember it by.

After she left, I got out my box of bits and pieces to add the photos to the things I kept meaning to put in my scrapbook at home one of these days. Then, as usual, I couldn't resist poking through the other items in the box. There was the announcement of my shop's opening and a photo of the storefront on the opening day. There was a picture of the sofa I was saving up to buy for the living room of my new apartment.

And there were newspaper clippings from four months ago. They all had headlines like WHERE'S PENE-LOPE? and WHATEVER HAPPENED TO MISS PIGGY?

It was as if I'd completely disappeared into thin air, according to the articles. I hadn't changed my name, I hadn't changed my hairstyle, nothing was different except for my missing snout. In a way, my mother had been right—I was a fad, a flavor of the month. But Annie had been right, too. I was still the same person.

Something else caught my eye, and I pulled out a fancy program. It was from the night I'd gone with Edward and our parents to the benefit concert. The last time I'd seen Max. His own name wasn't even in the program, but it didn't matter. It was my only souvenir. I allowed myself a melancholy moment of remembrance, but I replaced the program quickly before the tears could automatically well up in my eyes.

I forced myself instead to think about Edward. I hadn't seen him since our almost-wedding, and I wondered how he was. I'd sent back the engagement ring but he hadn't acknowledged it. I imagined he was still living at home, being bullied by his parents and feeling sorry for himself. Someday, I'd go and talk to him about how to break free and let go of all the sadness. I felt that I could call myself an authority when it came to self-imprisonment.

I wasn't in that position anymore. So much had changed for me in the past few months. The shop, of course. It was the perfect career for me. With my love and knowledge of plants and flowers, I was able to create something more than a standard florist's shop. People came to Penelope's Petals for unusual arrangements, exotic plants, and all the information they needed to care for them. I was starting to build up a reputation.

I moved out of my shabby furnished room and found a little apartment in Midtown, not far from Annie's. I visited my parents occasionally, but my social life was too busy to spend much time with them. I still had my friends from the Cloverdilly, and I'd made more. Once, I asked the bartender at the Cloverdilly whatever happened to the guy who used to clean the place, and he told me he didn't work there anymore, that he was traveling with a band. I was glad. Even though that meant I wouldn't see him around, it meant that he must be happy.

The bell at the door tinkled again, and I shoved the

box back in its drawer. "Hi!" I greeted Annie. "What are you doing here at this hour?"

"I'm working. You've got deliveries." She dropped a stack of thick envelopes and boxes on my counter. "How was dinner last night?"

I did my usual eye roll at the memory of my monthly dinner with the Wilherns. "Quiet. I still can't believe I'm able to describe an evening with my mother as quiet!"

Annie grinned. "She still can't talk?"

"She can whisper a little, but the doctors say she'll never be able to do much more than that."

"And they still don't know what caused her to lose her voice?"

"Have you ever tried convincing a doctor that someone's been cursed by a witch?"

The bell rang, and a little girl carrying a bag came in with an adult. "Trick or treat!" the child sang out.

I was prepared for this—I had a big bowl of candies right under the counter. But I was too startled by her disguise to reach for them right away. She wore the mask of a pig—and not an animal-pig. This mask had rosy cheeks, long eyelashes, and curly brown hair. And a snout.

"Happy Halloween," I said brightly. "Who are you supposed to be?"

"I'm Penelope!"

Annie and I exchanged looks. "That's . . . cute," I said, and dropped some candy into her bag.

"Can you believe that?" I asked Annie.

Laughing, Annie nodded. "Actually, she's the third Penelope I've seen today. Listen, do you have plans for tonight?"

"No, but aren't we a little old for trick-or-treating?"

"We're invited to a Halloween party. Some newspaper reporter I met. I forget his name but I've got the address. He lives in one of those singles' apartment complexes, and the whole building is throwing the party. He specifically told me to bring you."

"Really?" I frowned. I'd met a lot of reporters during my brief fame, but I hadn't actually become friendly with any of them. But a big Halloween party could be fun.

"Okay, but I don't have a costume," I told Annie.

"I'll pick us up some masks," she said. "See ya later."

After she left, I had customers, and more trick or treaters. There were goblins and witches and Spider-Men—and more Penelopes. One group in particular got my attention—six girls together, five of whom were wearing Penelope Pig masks. I passed out the candy to the giggling bunch, but I paused when I reached the one who was wearing a Snow White costume. She was the only one who didn't look happy.

"Is something wrong?" I asked her.

She pouted. "Everyone else is Penelope, and I'm just stupid Snow White."

I gave her extra candy. "Well, it's good to be different. Different can be beautiful. And you'll stand out in a crowd." They turned to leave, and I called out to her.

"Hey, Snow White."

She turned and looked back at me.

"You know the song Snow White sings in the movie? 'Some Day My Prince Will Come'?"

She nodded.

"Don't count on it," I said.

It wasn't until an hour later that I had a chance to go through the deliveries that Annie had dropped off. There were seeds I'd ordered, and a couple of vases, and there were some books on flower arrangements, but one thick envelope was unexpected.

There was no return address on the envelope. No mark showing what city it came from, either. There wasn't even a stamp. I opened it and pulled out a manila folder. The label on it read JOHNNY MARTIN.

Johnny Martin. It rang a bell. Where had I seen that name before? In my mind, an image of that jazz concert program appeared. I frowned, trying to figure out why. Then I opened the folder and began to read.

And it all started to make sense.

# Chapter Thirty-three

"I can't believe you bought these masks," I said to Annie as we approached the apartment building.

"Come on, they're funny!"

"I just hadn't planned on ever looking like this again." I had to admit, though, it was a cute idea. Annie and I were both wearing Penelope masks.

And we weren't the only ones at the party with them. As we made our way through the building's crowded recreation room, I spotted a number of pig-girls.

"This is bizarre," I whispered to Annie. "I haven't been in the news in months! People think I disappeared."

"That's why you've become a legend," Annie replied. "Like Amelia Earhart!"

It looked like a good party. There was food and decorations, and a floor space had been cleared for dancing. I was hungry and I wanted to hit the buffet table first, but Annie had other plans.

"I have to pee," she announced.

"I see restrooms over there," I told her.

"Yeah, but do you see the line? I can't hold it that long. Hey, there's the guy who invited us. Wait here." I watched as she went over to a man disguised as a pirate with an eye patch. They conferred for a moment, and then she came back.

"He says I can use the bathroom in his apartment. His roommate's there. Come with me, okay?"

I put my hunger on hold and left the room. We took the elevator and got off on the fourth floor.

"It's number 4D," Annie murmured. We reached the right door, and she rang the bell. A few seconds later, the door opened.

I caught my breath. I couldn't speak, I couldn't even breathe. Max was standing there.

"Yes?"

Annie spoke. "Your roommate said my friend here could use your bathroom."

He shrugged. "Yeah, okay."

Annie pushed me through the door. "Later, girl-friend." And she took off.

I just stood there, frozen, feeling like I'd just entered some alternate universe. Max pointed. "Bathroom's down the hall on the right."

"Thanks," I managed to say. Somehow, I made my legs work and went down the hall. Once inside the bathroom, I closed the door, put the seat down on the toilet, and just sat there for a minute. Then I got up, gripped the sink, and tried to collect my wits. I took deep breaths and raised my eyes to the mirror.

It was the first time I'd looked at myself since putting on the mask. I couldn't begin to describe how it felt, seeing myself like that, the way I used to look. The old me. Who'd been the real me. Which I still was, mask or no mask.

I had no idea how long I stood there, looking at myself, but I must have been in there a while because I heard him call, "You okay in there?"

I came out and went back into the living room. That was when I noticed the suitcase. "Are you going somewhere?" I asked.

"I'm moving."

My heart plummeted. "Far away?"

"Nah, just to my own apartment, around the corner. This was just temporary. Lemon let me move in till I got myself pulled together."

"And you're . . . all pulled together now?"

He didn't look at me while he spoke. "Yeah, I've got a job."

"Doing what?" I asked.

"I'm with a band."

"What do you play?"

"Piano. Listen, I don't want to be rude but I'm kind of busy. . . ."

"Why won't you look at me?" I blurted out.

He finally turned in my direction. "Sorry. It's the mask. I've been seeing that mask everywhere today, and it's getting on my nerves."

"What's wrong with it? Too ugly for you?"

He shook his head. "It's not that. It just . . . it reminds me of someone I used to know."

"Someone . . . someone you cared about?"

He busied himself with folding a shirt. "Yeah."

"A lot?"

He looked at me sharply. *"Yes."*

I blurted out the next question. "Then why aren't you with her now?"

This time he didn't look away. I had the feeling he *couldn't* look away, like his eyes were glued to my face / mask, like he could see through it, like he was searching for something. I was suddenly reminded of the way he'd looked in that mirror in the music room, as if he could see through it to me on the other side.

I repeated my question, more gently this time. "Why aren't you with her?"

"Because . . . because I wasn't good enough for her. She deserved better. I couldn't give her what she wanted."

My voice became a whisper. "What did she want?"

His gaze on me remained steady, penetrating. "To be free."

"She's free now, Max."

He moved closer, his eyes filled with wonder. "Penelope?" He put his arms around me, and I was very grateful that the mask didn't cover my lips. I wouldn't have been able to feel his kiss.

"Penelope," he murmured, his voice choking. "I love you. I always loved you, from the very beginning. But I can't break the curse."

"That's okay," I said. I stepped back and took off the mask. "It turns out that I could."

He looked like he was in shock.

"It's really me, Max."

"My name . . . it's not Max. It's Johnny."

"I know," I said. "I'm just not used to it yet. It's me, Johnny."

"Penelope . . ."

"Yes, I'm still Penelope."

He took me in his arms again.

"I always was," I whispered in his ear. "I was always Penelope. I just didn't know it."

"*I* did," he said. "I just didn't think that was enough for you."

"I had to learn that it was," I told him. "That's what lifted the curse, when I finally accepted myself. I used to think my life was a fairy tale, and I couldn't be happy until someone came along and turned me into the real

Penelope. But I was Penelope all the time, no matter what face I had. And I always will be."

He held me tightly, and I could feel magic all around us. And I knew that we would live happily ever after.